PUFFIN BOOKS

CLEAN BOWLED, BUTTERFINGERS!

Khyrunnisa A., prize-winning author of children's fiction, created the popular comic character Butterfingers for the children's magazine *Tinkle*. Her first two children's novels, *Howzzat Butterfingers!* (2010) and *Goal, Butterfingers!* (2012), were published by Puffin. *Clean Bowled, Butterfingers!* is the third in the Butterfingers series.

A book of short stories, *Lost in Ooty and Other Adventure Stories,* was brought out by Unisun Publications in 2010. Her stories also appear in *Tinkle, Dimdima* and other children's magazines. Some of her stories, for children and for adults, have been published in various anthologies by Puffin, Children's Book Trust and Unisun Publications.

She was a columnist for the *New Indian Express* and freelances for other publications. She has an ongoing fortnightly column, 'Inside View', in the *Hindu Metroplus.*

She worked as Associate Professor of English at All Saints' College, Trivandrum, and is now a full-time writer. She can be reached at khyrubutter@yahoo.com.

'*Khyrunnisa does it again with this latest instalment of the Butterfingers saga.* Clean Bowled *is amusingly written, imaginatively plotted and always delightful, with martinet principals, jewel thieves, smelly gloves, exploding sapotas and an exciting cricketing climax. Wish I could be a kid again to savour the fun even more!*'

Dr Shashi Tharoor

Also in Puffin by Khyrunnisa A.

Howzzat Butterfingers!
Goal, Butterfingers!

KHYRUNNISA A.

PUFFIN BOOKS

PUFFIN BOOKS
Published by the Penguin Group
Penguin Books India Pvt. Ltd, 7th Floor, Infinity Tower C, DLF Cyber City,
Gurgaon 122 002, Haryana, India
Penguin Group (USA) Inc., 375 Hudson Street, New York, New York 10014, USA
Penguin Group (Canada), 90 Eglinton Avenue East, Suite 700, Toronto, Ontario,
M4P 2Y3, Canada
Penguin Books Ltd, 80 Strand, London WC2R 0RL, England
Penguin Ireland, 25 St Stephen's Green, Dublin 2, Ireland (a division of Penguin
Books Ltd)
Penguin Group (Australia), 707 Collins Street, Melbourne, Victoria 3008, Australia
Penguin Group (NZ), 67 Apollo Drive, Rosedale, Auckland 0632, New Zealand
Penguin Books (South Africa) (Pty) Ltd, Block D, Rosebank Office Park,
181 Jan Smuts Avenue, Parktown North, Johannesburg 2193, South Africa

Penguin Books Ltd, Registered Offices: 80 Strand, London WC2R 0RL, England

First published in Puffin by Penguin Books India 2015

ISBN 9780143333364

Typeset in Sabon by Manipal Digital Systems, Manipal
Printed at Thomson Press India Ltd, New Delhi

A PENGUIN RANDOM HOUSE COMPANY

For all my students,
who have taught me so much . . .

Contents

1

A Rainy Monday

Rumble! Crackle! Boom! Mr Rajeev Kishen, entering the dining room for breakfast, gave a start as the sudden light-and-sound effect produced by the approaching storm took him unawares. He was better prepared, though, for what happened next.

Bang! Crash! 'Oops!' announced the arrival of his son, Amar. 'Not my fault, Dad, Ma!' said Amar, looking down ruefully at the wreck of a glass vase that he had knocked off the side table when he burst into the room with his customary speed and inaccuracy. 'It's the storm's fault. The wind blew the curtain into my face and . . .'

'You couldn't see where you were going, so you walked into the table instead of around it,' Mr Kishen completed the story for him. 'Haven't we heard variations of this before?' But he was secretly pleased; he had always hated the vase.

Amar's mother, Shreya Kishen, had rushed into the room when she heard the noise and, anticipating the accident, had brought along the broom and the dustpan that stood handy for just such an emergency, and there were emergencies aplenty in a house that had Amar in it. 'Get out of my way!' she issued a crisp order as, with an expertise born out of regular practice, she swept the area that had been recently bombed by the vase. 'But what's this?' She held up a plain piece of glass, looking at it as a detective might a fingernail among the bloodstains. The vase had been a hideous blue.

'I had taken some water up to drink last night and was bringing the empty glass down,' Amar confessed sheepishly.

'Well, you did a thorough job of bringing it down all right,' summed up Mr Kishen. 'Forever Butterfingers!'

Thirteen-year-old Amar Kishen was naturally butterfingered. He seemed to have been born with the knack for dropping things and had polished his slippery grip skills so early on in life that the nickname 'Butterfingers' or 'Butter' for short was as inevitable as the wreckage he strewed around him. His long-suffering father had bestowed the name on him and everyone who knew Amar commended its suitability.

Amar maintained a diplomatic silence while the room continued to resonate with the sounds of the storm outside. As the family finally sat down to breakfast, Amar broke his self-imposed vow of silence. 'I've been thinking,' he pronounced.

His father, buried behind the newspaper, heard this and raised his head to remark, 'Thinking? Excellent! I should've guessed the storm was a portent of something unusual. Never too late to begin, son. So, what has your mind thought up?'

Amar ignored this and began again, but with a slight variation, 'I've been studying . . .'

'This is just getting better and better,' his father interrupted, this time from behind the paper.

Now the words tumbled out from Amar, '. . . the calendar and find it'll soon be six months since Colonel Nadkarni passed away. I thought it'd be very nice if we could . . .'

'Could what?' prompted his mother, when Amar paused to breathe.

'Well, I mean, if we could do something special to remember him by,' Amar concluded rather tamely.

The late Colonel Nadkarni had been the owner of the playground of Amar's school, The Green Park Higher Secondary School. He had always been a great cricket enthusiast. Affectionately called Colonel Uncle by the students, he had shared a great rapport with them and his sudden death had left the whole school grief-stricken. Amar and his friends, to whom Colonel Nadkarni had been something of a mentor and a close friend, had been heartbroken.

'Like what?' asked Mr Kishen, putting the paper down. 'Play another cricket match, if I know you, and . . .'

'Spot on, Dad!' Amar cut in to express his approval. His father did have his inspired moments. 'I was thinking we could have a commemorative cricket match.'

'. . . I'm sure, if your principal has any sense, he'll not allow it,' Mr Kishen completed what he was saying. 'I'm all with the Sporting Thief; burning cricket equipment is a great social service he's rendering. He's done it again.'

'Again? Where, Dad?' Amar, who had stood up to fetch a hot puri from the kitchen, now abandoned that pursuit and changed direction to take swift, panther-like leaps and secure a vantage position behind his father that offered him a good view of the news item Mr Kishen had mentioned. He peered over his father's shoulder to scan the paper eagerly, quite oblivious to his mother's annoyed order, 'Amar! Sit down and finish your breakfast!'

'But here it says "Jewel Thief Escapes". Where did this character spring from? Where's what you said about the Sporting Thief?'

'Will you stop sending your volcanic eruptions down my neck, Amar?' Mr Kishen exploded. At that moment the clock began to chime.

'Goodness, it's nine already! I'm going to be late!' Mr Kishen dropped the paper and quickly gulped down his coffee.

'I'll be late too, Ma, very late. I'll miss my bus anyway,' Amar said in a plaintive tone, leaping back to his chair and snatching a cold puri en route. You can't be too choosy when you've run out of time. As another loud clap of thunder filled the room, he looked significantly at his mother. 'It's beginning to rain and looks like it'll be impressive stuff. I'm sure to get drenched. Today's a half-day anyway; don't know the reason. Who wants to go on a rainy half-day? I bet many teachers will take leave and . . .'

'So it would be a wonderful idea to spend the whole day at home? Good plan, Amar,' Mr Kishen broke in.

4

'Unfortunately, here's the spoiler. Half-day or whole day, you're going to school. I'm taking you there. I'll drop you, though it will delay me even further. And don't worry about your teachers' plans. Go on, get ready, quick, and be down in five minutes.'

The Kishen residence turned into a maelstrom of frenetic activity for the next few minutes. Mr Kishen took rapid, giant strides and disappeared into his room, Mrs Kishen darted back to the kitchen to get her son's lunch ready while Amar charged towards the bathroom, almost knocking over a chair that stood undecided on one leg for a few seconds before it settled in favour of recovering its balance rather than toppling over. The newspaper was forgotten in the mad rush to beat the clock.

The car wouldn't start, raising fresh hope within Amar, but then coughed and wheezed and treacherously came to life. Amar's mother closed the gate after the car left and returning to the house that had fallen quiet, took deep breaths to calm herself, as her yoga instructor had advised. Feeling relaxed now, she took up the abandoned newspaper and settled down to read the reports on the Jewel Thief and the Sporting Thief.

The surge of traffic as the car approached the school gate forced Mr Kishen to lower the speed to a crawl. Amar, looking out anxiously for his friends, spotted Kiran and yelled to his father, 'Stop here, Dad! There's Kiran.' Rolling down the window he shouted,

'Hey Tub!' then turned to his father and said, 'I'll go with him. And what luck, he actually has an umbrella!'

His father, who had instinctively applied the brakes with an angry, half-expressed curse when Amar had almost blown his ear off with his yell, snapped, 'Call that an umbrella? Good luck with it. Bye, Amar. Hey, don't forget your bag!'

Amar, who had leapt out to join his friend, gave a reverse leap intending to yank his bag out and bang shut the car door with it in one ambitious movement. The bag got stuck. His cheerful, 'Bye, Dad, thanks for dropping me!' ended with the characteristic 'Oops!' as he pulled free the bag only to drop it, with unerring precision, straight into a puddle.

Mr Kishen grimaced, leaned over to close the door and started the engine, not wishing to witness anything further. Discretion was often for him the better part of valour when it came to matters involving Amar. Mr Kishen's aim that morning had been to see that his son didn't skip school. He had achieved that purpose and didn't want to add to his good deeds by taking a soggy son, his soggy bag, his soggy friend with a soggy headgear that masqueraded as an umbrella to the school's doorstep, an endeavour that would set him back by a good twenty minutes. He sped away, sending a goodbye wave of water over the boys. With some luck at the traffic lights, he might manage to reach his office on time after all.

A Rainy Monday

Amar retrieved his wet canvas bag and patting it as if his hand was a piece of blotting paper that would absorb the water the bag had soaked up, took shelter under his friend's umbrella, only to discover why his father had made those uncharitable remarks. There are umbrellas and umbrellas, and then there was Kiran's umbrella. Two of its ribs, broken and dangling down, threatened to stab Amar in the eye whenever he chanced to look up. The runner, well named, ran down every time they tried to keep it up, so that the umbrella kept closing on its own. Worse, the canopy had been made of a material that had Welcome to Water written all over it and was hardly any protection for the boys' heads.

'Do you really think this is an umbrella?' Amar asked reproachfully. 'Might as well throw it away. Useless thing!'

'Ha, it was thrown away. I picked it up from the dustbin at home. Couldn't find any other.'

Abandoning the umbrella for the marginally better protection of his bag, Amar placed it over his head and took off crying, 'Race you to school!' Kiran huffed and puffed gamely after him, the umbrella flapping like a bewitched hat on his head. Physically and temperamentally, Kiran was the antithesis of Amar. While Amar was tall, thin and driven by restless energy, Kiran was short, stocky and laid-back. His nickname, Tub, was perfect not only because he was constructed like one, but also because Amar, his closest friend, was frequently called Butter or But for short and Tub was

7

But reversed. The two were often referred to as But-Tub. Kiran good-humouredly said he was designed to catch whatever his taller friend dropped.

Though the bell had long gone, the scene at the entrance when Amar and Kiran arrived was still chaotic. Boys were talking at the top of their voices with the pitch going higher and higher to make themselves heard. Some students were trying half-heartedly to close their umbrellas, more keen to see how many of their friends they could jab in the process. Some were taking off their raincoats with such a flourish they were able to send satisfying sprays of water like garden sprinklers all about them. The ones who had balanced their bags as shields against the rain were now looking ruefully at the consequences of that decision. Those who hadn't bothered about any defence at all, regretted the bravado that had left them so thoroughly wet. And suddenly, over all this noise came a voice that boomed like thunder with a blocked nose. Yet it was distinctive enough to be recognized as belonging to the principal, Mr Jagmohan. And clearly he had a cold.

'Go do your glasses! Ibbediately!' Everybody fell silent, though there were a couple of suppressed giggles from the younger boys. Soon all that could be heard was the sound of squelchy shoes as their owners slid, slipped and struggled to navigate with as much speed as possible over the slippery floor and up the stairs to reach their respective classrooms.

Shyam sir, the careworn class teacher of VIII A, was already in class when Amar, Kiran, Ajay and Eric dashed in, making enough noise to sound like elephants on the warpath.

'Sorry we're late, sir. May we enter? It's because of the rain! ' said Amar, speaking for all the latecomers.

Mr Shyam sighed. The class had been unusually nice and quiet in the proverbial calm before the storm mode. He decided to inject some humour into his welcome. 'Do you wish to enter because of the rain or are you late because of the rain?'

'Or does he wish to enter because he is late? You've left out that inference, sir, which is the third conclusion you can arrive at if you apply logic to the sequence of Butter's sentences,' said Kishore, the language buff.

'That will do, Kishore. No need to display your acumen for logic so early in the morning,' said Mr Shyam curtly. 'And get in quickly, boys, don't drip water at the entrance, someone might slip.'

Prophetic words, for a couple of sneezes heralded the arrival of another student who literally slithered into the classroom. Arjun, the guitar-playing eccentric, was making a dramatic entrance, his long hair sticking to his neck like a rat's scraggy tail. Mr Shyam, who for all his brusque manner had a kind heart, was concerned and put out a hand to halt the boy's headlong progress and they danced like two out-of-practice ballet dancers before recovering their balance. 'You are so wet! And you have a cold! We should get you dry. Why don't you go to the sickroom?'

'I'll take him there, sir!' There was an eager chorus. The students were ever willing to help one another, especially when the assistance involved any movement away from the classroom. Much as Mr Shyam would have loved to let the whole class accompany Arjun to the sickroom and leave him in peace in an empty classroom, he knew he was wishing for the impossible.

Eric had been made class leader just the previous week and it was only proper that he should be given the responsibility, and since he was almost as wet as Arjun, it made even better sense to do that. 'Eric, take him there, and get yourself dry too.'

As the two boys left the class, Amar asked, 'What about me, sir?' Then he whispered to Kishore seated next to him, 'Is it me or I?' The use of the first person pronoun always troubled Amar.

'Me,' whispered Kishore.

'Well, what about you?' Mr Shyam asked.

'Me am, I mean, I am wet too.'

'So? Almost everyone here is wet, me included. We'll all get dry soon, not to worry. It stands to reason that we will. Now listen to me.'

'A dry lecture!' sighed Kishore and whispered to Amar, 'by the way, heard about the Sporting Thief's latest?'

'No! I've been dying to know! Dad mentioned something was in the paper, but before I . . .'

'Stop whispering, both of you,' said Mr Shyam, annoyed, and sent a piece of coloured chalk in their direction. Amar put his book up defensively and flicked it to the leg side, and it went sailing to the door to hit someone who had just arrived with an 'Excuse me, sir . . .'

'Oh, I'm sorry,' apologized Mr Shyam, glaring at Amar, before he took another look at the new entrant and exclaimed in surprise, 'Reshmi! You!'

'Reshmi!' The whole class echoed, in happy surprise.

'Yes, Shyam sir.' She beamed. Looking at the others, she held up the chalk and said, 'I took the catch, when it bounced off my nose!'

'Hahaha!' Everyone laughed, except Mr Shyam, who sighed and said, 'Have you come to visit us? Fine day you've chosen!'

'Not visit, sir, I'm rejoining this class.'

'What!' Mr Shyam looked astonished. Reshmi continued, 'My parents had to go abroad on a project and didn't want me to be in the hostel of Il Paradiso School. I like this place and since my father had got to know Mr Jagmohan because I once stayed with Princi, I mean the principal, he asked Jagmohan sir if I could study in this school for some time. Anyways, here I am! May I come in, sir?'

She grinned at the class and the students grinned back. Mr Shyam's face fell.

Reshmi and three other girls had come to Green Park School on an exchange programme a couple of months back. She and a girl called Sonanda, aka Sony,

11

had been placed in VIII A which had Minu Sippy, the only girl in the school, on its rolls. Minu's father was a famous lepidopterist who had come to the town some time back to study the butterflies there. Since his assignment would take him a few months, he had brought his family along and as a special consideration, Mr Jagmohan had admitted Minu into his school.

Mr Shyam had been quite indignant that his quirky crew of students that consisted of Amar, Arjun, Kishore and Thomas, should now include these new girls too. Reshmi had been the more mischievous of the two and Shyam sir had been quite relieved when the programme had ended. And now here she was, back like a homing pigeon and grinning from ear to ear as she threw the chalk back at Amar.

'Of course, of course! Welcome back, Reshmi,' Mr Shyam said with a forced smile. 'You may sit there, achoo!' he sneezed, pointing to the seat left empty by Arjun. What a day! And he seemed to have caught a cold too. Was it possible for Arjun to have given him the germs so quickly? That boy was capable of anything! Mr Shyam suddenly felt ill and tired. If only he could leave the class. But his guardian angel was, as usual, in deep slumber. Or so he stoically told himself when the intercom crackled and Mr Jagmohan's voice came floating over.

'All the teachers are requested to assemble in the common staffroom immediately. Please come here after assigning the students some work.'

Roars of joy rose from every classroom; Class VIII A's were the loudest. Amar whispered to Kishore, 'I think Princi's got his nose unblocked.'

'Yes, he spoke intelligibly. Must have been helped by some solid sneezing,' laughed Kishore. 'How I'd love to witness a proper sneezing fit!'

It was a morning when wishes came true because Mr Shyam promptly obliged, sneezing seven times in a row, thankfully stopping when the students began to count them aloud.

'Read those chapters,' he told the class.

'Which chapters, sir?' asked Kiran.

'Any,' he said, adding unconvincingly, 'and keep quiet.' He had hardly taken a few steps from the class, when a tidal wave of noise reached his ears. He hastened towards the common staffroom, sneezing all the way.

2

Amar's Sublime Idea

A volley of questions came Reshmi's way as soon as Mr Shyam left. 'I'll field them all, one by one,' she said, as if facing a television interview, 'not to worry, and anyways . . .'

'Ha, somebody's back to her bad old "anyways" ways,' said Kishore, disapprovingly. He thought he had managed to get her out of the habit when she had been an exchange student two months back. 'Looks like I'll have to start from scratch.'

'Are you staying with Princi?' asked Amar. He could never get over the fact that Reshmi had lodged briefly in Mr Jagmohan's house.

'No, no,' said Reshmi. 'I'm staying with some family friends. But enough about me, what's all this I hear about a Sporting Thief in your town? Sony and I kept discussing it. You people have all the fun. We lead such a boring life in Il Paradiso.'

'In a school named Il Paradiso, you shouldn't be seeking excitement,' teased Ajay.

'The Sporting Thief, the Sporting Thief! Tell me about him! Our papers only gave one-line reports. Why don't we look for him? In fact, that's the reason I wanted to come here.'

'And here we thought it's because you were pining for our company!' Ajay winked.

'I'll tell you all we know about the Sporting Thief,' said Amar. 'Then I'll tell you all about another idea I have.'

'We're in trouble!' said Eric, who had just entered the class.

'Why, what's wrong with Arjun?' asked Amar, looking concerned.

'Not much. I meant we're in trouble because I can't think of any idea of yours that hasn't landed us in a soup.'

'Not this one; this is one supercool idea. You'll kick yourselves for not having thought of it.'

'And then kick you for having thought of it,' said Ajay.

Amar cleared his throat and began, 'Reshmi, the newspapers gave him the name "Sporting Thief". Ironic, if you ask me. We sometimes call this guy the Unsporting Thief, that's what he actually is.'

But before he could elaborate, Minu gave a shriek. 'Hey, look here!' She waved a paper she had snatched from Jayaram. 'Jay's written a poem about the Unsporting Thief!'

Jayaram, blushing as he always did when the secret lyrical side of his nature was exposed, tried to wrest the paper from her, but Kishore pre-empted him. Kishore vaulted on to the teacher's table holding the paper aloft, while Kiran and Arvind held Jayaram back and scrolling his eyes quickly down the poem, commented, 'This is not bad. Not bad at all. So our Jay was occupying his time fruitfully while Shyam sir droned on about er . . . whatever. Listen, everybody!' Kishore cleared his throat, waved his arms theatrically and having secured everyone's attention, began:

The Unsporting Thief

We seek him here, we seek him there,
The police seek him everywhere,
But the Sporting Thief, to be fair
Just disappears into thin air.
He works in the night
Sometimes by moonlight
Breaks into many a shed
When people are snug in bed.
But it's not gold he's after
That's what makes it much dafter;
It's bats and pads and stumps and gloves
These are the things he really loves.
But wait a minute, does he really love them
When he doesn't treat them as he should a gem?
That sneaky, secretive cricket-hater
Puts them in a heap a little later.
He sets fire to them; we cry out in grief,
'End the arson, you damned elusive Unsporting Thief!'

'Wow!' exclaimed Amar in admiration. 'Awesome, man!'

'Yes, I couldn't have put it better myself,' said Kishore pompously, 'although the number of metrical feet in the penultimate line isn't . . .'

'Metrical feet, my foot!' Eric held Kishore by his feet and, dragging him down from his pedestal, dumped him on the floor. Kiran and Amar promptly sat on him.

'Pffft, ok. I was only joking,' Kishore gasped as he pushed the boys off and struggled to his feet. He joined the whole class in a big round of applause for the budding poet. Kiran and Arvind thumped Jayaram on his back warmly.

Thomas, also called Doubting Thomas by his friends because of his love for asking questions, looked very thoughtful. '"We seek him here, we seek him there . . ." Where have I heard it before?'

'*The Scarlet Pimpernel*, silly!' said Eric. 'It was in our suggested reading list last year. I suppose your mind has gone back to its tabula rasa state, haha!'

'Now Reshmi, that is, in a poetic nutshell, the story of the Sporting or Unsporting Thief,' said Amar. 'But we can't understand why he's doing this.'

'I bet it's a deep-seated phobia firmly embedded in his unconscious.' Kishore looked serious as he explained his theory. 'His ambitious father, who was a devotee of Sachin Tendulkar, probably put pads on his legs when he had just learnt to walk, placed a cricket bat in his right hand and at gunpoint ordered him to whack the ball he bowled. And thus began the poor guy's hatred of cricket and everything connected with it. He must have been a left-hander to boot, and that triggered off a personality disorder. There's always a psychological reason behind every action of a man. Actually . . .'

'That's enough of your learned psychoanalysis, Kishore!' Amar said, impatiently. 'And how did the father manage to bowl while pointing a gun at the same time? Idiot!'

'And obviously Kishore's father regularly sat on his head when he was a baby and that's why Kishore's brains got addled. Psychological and physiological reasons,' put in Ajay.

'Think he's a pyromaniac who seeks novelty in the raw material?' Minu mused.

'Likely. But how come the police haven't been able to nab him?' asked Reshmi.

'I bet they haven't tried at all. Which policeman would bother about sporting equipment unless it belonged to somebody like Tendulkar or Dhoni? Remember how Sanju Samson's sports trophies were stolen, but the police didn't do much about it,' said Kiran.

'By the way, what did the Sporting Thief do yesterday?' asked Amar eagerly. 'What was the newspaper report about?'

'Ah, the usual stuff,' Kishore explained. 'The police found a couple of burnt bats and stumps in the empty field behind Shakti Theatre and they think it could be the equipment that went missing from the National Sports Club last week.'

'And don't forget the new entrant into this group of thieves, the Jewel Thief!' exclaimed Amar. 'I saw the headline in the papers.'

'Totally unconnected,' opined Kishore sagely. 'He escaped only yesterday. So he can't be the same Sporting Thief. Our man has been at it for a couple of months now.'

'But the Jewel Thief's interesting, all the same. I managed to read the bit about him in the morning,' said Minu. 'He's an expert thief of precious gems, though diamonds are his weakness. He's a slippery customer but the police finally managed to arrest him a few months back. Yesterday he escaped from prison. So now that they have the juicy case of a jewel thief, the police have a good excuse not to bother about the sports gear hater.'

'Yep! So he's all ours.' Amar rubbed his hands with glee. 'Cool! Let's see how we can find him. But before we make those plans, let me tell you my sublime idea.'

'Sublime?' Kishore looked disbelieving. 'What idea of yours can ever be called sublime? Subterranean, substandard, subhuman, sub . . .'

'Subside, you ass. Enough of your wisecracks. Everybody listen to my diamond gem of an idea!' Amar banged the table hard. 'Do you realize that in two weeks it will be six months since Colonel Uncle passed away?'

The mere mention of Colonel Nadkarni was enough to sober everyone down. They now gave Amar their complete attention and he continued, gratified that his announcement had the desired effect. 'I was thinking that we should commemorate the six month anniversary. What's it called?'

'Actually, there's no specific word for that,' said Kishore. 'And though, to be precise, anniversary means observing or commemorating something that took place in a previous year since "ann" derives from the Latin "annum" meaning "year", these days it is acceptable to say three month anniversary and so on. It's a mistaken notion to believe that the meaning of words must directly reflect their etymology. That's known as "the etymological fallacy". If, however, you want to be really accurate, you could use "sixth monthiversary" or "sixth mensiversary" or even "semi-anniversary" though they sound awkward and haven't gained currency yet . . .'

Amar's head reeled. 'What are you blathering on about? I asked you a simple question and you go on like a textbook about currency notes and stuff!'

'I only gave you the answer,' Kishore grinned. He loved to demonstrate his knowledge and his flair for words. 'Anyway, go on.'

'Why don't we organize a commemorative cricket match to honour Colonel Uncle's memory? He loved cricket so much; it'd be the right thing for the occasion.'

The idea was greeted with great enthusiasm by his classmates.

'Awesome plan, Butter!'

'Great!'

'Can't believe you thought of that one!'

'Excellent!'

'Wonderful! You do have your moments!'

'Er, sublime!' conceded Kishore.

Amar grinned, pleased. The next step was the difficult one of obtaining permission. Amar knew from past experience that the task would be dumped on him; he knew his friends too well. And he wasn't wrong. The others began by discussing the reasons why the good idea might well be turned down. After all, they had already spent a lot of time on sports that year. They had played the matches of the annual Colonel Nadkarni Under-15 Inter School Cricket Tournament, followed by the football 'World Cup' and a few tennis matches too. Mr Jagmohan was bound to veto the proposal, fond as he had been of Colonel Nadkarni.

'It's Amar for permission!' announced Eric, speaking for the whole class. He was taking his duties as class leader quite seriously, though it didn't extend to approaching Mr Jagmohan for anything if he could help it.

'Of course, it has to be you, Butter!' agreed Kiran. 'But I'll come along if you want,' he added gallantly. After all, being best friends warranted such volunteering, though Kiran hoped the offer would be turned down. But Amar turned to him gratefully.

'Thanks, man. Shall we go now? Is this the right time? What's today's half-day in aid of? Does anyone know? Sounded very urgent, the way Princi summoned all the teachers.'

'I heard there's a general meeting of the staff with the trustees in the afternoon, or at least that's what Shekhar Uncle told me in the morning,' said Arun.

21

Shekhar, whom the students called Shekhar Uncle, was Mr Jagmohan's peon and the friend, ally and saviour of Amar and his friends. He fed them with inside information, warned them about impending danger and often got them out of trouble, though there was a limit to how much he could help where Amar's misadventures were concerned. On those occasions, Shekhar's was a comforting presence when the errant boys were sent to detention.

'Then he's bound to be very busy and would be furious if you go to him with such a proposal at this time,' said Jayaram.

'Yes,' agreed Minu, who often erred on the side of caution. 'Wait till tomorrow.'

'No, no, no,' protested Amar. 'There's no time like a busy time to get the nod from Princi. He'd be so preoccupied, he'll give his consent without being aware of it.'

'Right you are! There's a tide in the affairs of men . . .' began Kishore.

'Storms and tides later,' said Amar airily, and dragged Kiran out of the classroom.

Mr Jagmohan was a worried man as he sniffed and snuffled. No, it wasn't his cold that was troubling him, though it did add to his woes, but the impending meeting of the trustees with the staff. In fact, he had been taken completely by surprise when he received an email the previous week from Mr Vijay Singh, the chairman of the board of trustees of the school, famous for calling a spade a double-headed tomahawk. It was in his characteristically abrupt style:

My dear Jagmohan, why are your teachers always falling sick? I've not heard such nonsense in my life. I'm shocked by the number of letters forwarded to me requesting sanction of leave on medical grounds and the mountain of medical bills for reimbursement submitted along with them. This is just not acceptable. You seem to have a reprehensible talent for choosing the unhealthiest people to fill the teaching posts.

Mr Jagmohan bristled with indignation on reading this, a state of mind that was immediately expressed in a coughing fit. How very unfair! It was always the board that made the final decision in appointing teachers; he was more an ornament at these interviews than anything else. And now he was being blamed for deliberately hand-picking germ-infested teachers!

The teachers at Green Park seem to be a particularly fragile bunch whose resistance to illness is almost non-existent. Something must be done. How can a school function well if its teachers are sickly and always on leave? I think it's because you haven't introduced the sporting

culture in the school, Jagmohan. The staff just don't
exercise enough. All work and no play makes teachers a sick
lot. They have to build resistance. There's nothing
like sports to make people fit. I'm glad you at least
are healthy.

Mr Jagmohan gave a guilty start and as if on cue,
his nose tingled, the warning sign of an impending
sneeze. He tried to stifle it by pressing his nose tight
with his thumb and index finger, but only succeeded
in orchestrating a sneeze so explosive that the room
rocked. Shekhar came flying into the room to find out
if a gun had been let off there.

We, the trustees, have decided to meet you and the
teachers personally to thrash out this issue. We must
take vital decisions for their well-being. Please make
arrangements for the meeting on Monday afternoon and
see that all, even the sickest, are present.

Mr Jagmohan kept putting off sharing this email with
his teachers, merely telling them that the trustees wished
to discuss some serious issues with them at a meeting
on Monday afternoon, a meeting so important that
the school was being given a half holiday. Attendance
was compulsory, he said, whether the teachers were in
wheelchairs or on stretchers. That stirred the curiosity
of the staff and there was wide private speculation on
the real purpose of the meeting. Quite a few found the

summons ominous, while some naive teachers who were given to romantic illusions actually thought their services to the school were going to be rewarded with a huge raise in salary and that the chairman wished to personally convey the good news to them. They began dreaming of exotic vacations with their families.

On Monday morning, Mr Jagmohan decided it was time to sound the teachers out about what would be discussed at the meeting. So he made the announcement requesting them to come to the common staffroom. But before addressing them, he thought it would be wise to consult Mr Sunderlal, the sports master, not only because the principal valued his suggestions but because the discussion was to do with what Mr Sunderlal was an expert at. Mr Jagmohan sent for the sports teacher. Shekhar accompanied Mr Sunderlal into the room and lingered there, pretending to be busy doing inconsequential tasks. Shekhar liked to be well informed about all that was happening in the school and this was how he generally achieved that purpose.

Amar and Kiran reached the principal's room and heard voices inside. 'I don't think we should go in now, Butter.' Kiran looked uncertain.

'Sounds like Princi's busy. This IS the right time,' Amar reassured his friend, and knocked on the door.

When there was no summons from inside, he kept up a steady drumming on the door. Carried away by the rhythm, he was trying to create a new tune when an angry voice yelled, 'Who's that idiot?

Stop that racket and come in!' Kiran wisely chose to remain hidden outside as Mr Jagmohan exclaimed, 'Amar! I should have known! What's the problem? How many times have I asked you not to disturb me when I'm busy unless it is something very serious?'

'This is very serious, Mr Jagmohan. This is to do with Colonel Uncle, I mean Colonel Nadkarni.'

Mr Sunderlal looked up with interest. 'It's a good thing you are here too, Mr Sunderlal,' Amar continued. 'Do you know, sirs, it will soon be six months since Colonel Nadkarni passed away? We were thinking we could have a cricket match to honour his memory and . . .'

'You came to tell me this, you foolish boy, while I am discussing something very important with Sunderlal? And who gave you permission to leave your classroom? You have absolutely no sense of propriety, no sense of anything, no sense at all. Go away!' Mr Jagmohan gave Amar a furious glare. But the boy stood his ground. This was how it often worked.

'Sir, it's just one match. Between two Green Park teams. Sir, please . . .'

'Get lost, Amar!' Mr Jagmohan stood up and came to him with an angry roar (its effect somewhat diminished when he stopped short to sneeze twice), caught Amar by the scruff of his neck and led him out of the room. Amar managed to dart a look of mute appeal towards Mr Sunderlal as he was roughly shepherded out. 'Go on, disappear! ' Mr Jagmohan shouted to make himself clearer and, catching sight of Kiran, added, 'Both of you!' before slamming the door. Kiran was happy to obey and ran back to the class but Amar stayed behind. It was well known that once he had set his mind on something, Amar wouldn't rest until he had seen it through.

'He's nuts! I bet he's going to get into deep trouble,' Kiran told his friends in class.

But Amar was made of sterner stuff. He remained there hoping to try his luck once again when the principal left the room. He also hoped the telling look of appeal he gave Mr Sunderlal would have its desired effect. It had. Inside the room, Mr. Sunderlal said to Mr Jagmohan, 'Actually, Amar's idea is good. After all, Nadkarni did such a lot for the school.'

'Hrrmph!' Mr Jagmohan gave one of his special grunts, almost as famous as his glares. He sounded unconvinced.

'By the way, Mr Jagmohan, the latch of the shed where we keep the sports equipment needs to be repaired. It doesn't fall and I can't lock the door. I'm worried because . . .'

'Later, later, Sunderlal,' the principal said impatiently. 'First things first. Coming back to what I was telling you, how do you think we should break the news to the teachers?'

Amar paced the corridor, already making plans in his head for the commemorative match. A little later Shekhar came out, followed by Mr Jagmohan and Mr Sunderlal. It was time for the staff meeting and while

Shekhar went in one direction, the other two walked in the direction away from Amar. Amar ran after them and catching up with the principal, asked again, 'Sir, don't you think it's a good idea? Colonel Uncle always loved sports, especially cricket.'

Mr Jagmohan was so sick of the word 'sports' that he turned angrily on the boy. 'You still here? Didn't I ask you to go away? And don't you dare mention the word "sports" to me!'

'Then what about the match, sir?' Amar persisted irrepressibly, though even his natural optimism was slowly beginning to wane.

'I've no time to listen to you now, Amar. Put your plan down on paper and I'll see. Now go!'

'Where shall I put it, sir?' asked Amar, brightening.

'Didn't I say on paper, boy? Can't you understand simple English?'

'Sir, I meant, where should I put the paper with the plan?'

'On the table,' squeaked Mr Jagmohan. His throat was beginning to trouble him. He noticed Amar open his mouth to ask 'which table' and forestalling him, spoke impatiently, 'My table, the staffroom table, the seminar hall table, the boardroom table, the classroom table, your bedroom table, the timetable, any table. Now just GO!'

Amar went, joy propelling him like a breeze towards his classroom. He had cleared the first hurdle in getting permission.

3

A Mix-up

Amar, vindicated in his belief that he had chosen the right time to wheedle permission of sorts out of Mr Jagmohan, jauntily entered the class to describe the success of his mission and found his friends listening to Shekhar with great amusement. Eric spotted him and shouted, 'Hey, Amar, you're missing something! Come, listen to this! It's just too funny! Do you know why the trustees are having a meeting with the teachers? Shekhar Uncle says it's because the board thinks our teachers fall sick too easily and therefore need to build up their stamina. They are going to discuss how to make the staff healthy. It seems there's a proposal they play more sports. What fun!'

'What? No wonder Princi blew his top when I mentioned sports to him. He snarled, "Don't you dare mention the word 'sports' to me!" I wondered what was wrong with him.'

'Did you tell him, "Be a good sport, Princi dear, and give us permission to play sports. That'd be really sporting of you. And know what? There's absolutely no sport like cricket"?' asked Jayaram, with a wink.

'Wonder how Princi is briefing the teachers about this,' giggled Reshmi. 'How I'd love to be there.'

'Oh, no!' exclaimed Shekhar in dismay. 'That reminds me! Mr Jagmohan told me to see to the chairs in the staffroom. I forgot!' And he scooted off.

He reached the staffroom to find it more silent than a tomb. The meeting had already begun. 'Take your seats!' Mr Jagmohan had said on entering the room and a shortage of chairs forced the latecomers to obey him literally by scampering to nearby rooms to get some seats. They quickly lugged what chairs they could find into the staffroom. The principal, looking decidedly awkward, had cleared his throat, sniffed a bit and begun uncertainly.

'Ahem, er, aargh, uh, um, ah, hmm . . .' The humming and hawing had the desired effect. Everyone had turned to him, curious. Having run out of non-lexical vocables, as Ms Philo, the English teacher, or Kishore, would have been quick to point out, he had plunged into the crux of the matter, unconsciously running his hand over his well-spread paunch and jiggling it as if it were a big blob of jelly. 'The reason why the trustees wish to meet you is because they are unhappy about the frequent sick leave you've been taking and the medical bills you've submitted. They think you are all unhealthy and wish to talk to you about how to get back in shape. They want you all to get interested in sports and play games regularly in order to become fit.'

Phew! There! He had got it out and now tried to tuck in his stomach by holding his breath. The effort resulted in a sneezing fit, and he emerged from it with tears in his eyes to find that he had been making all the noise in the room. The others were sullenly silent. That was when Shekhar appeared at the door.

'Where were you, Shekhar?' Mr Jagmohan snapped at him, secretly relieved that a whipping boy had been delivered at the doorstep as if on a wish. 'I'd asked you expressly to get everything ready here and this is when you appear! Bah!' The exclamation suited his mood and liking the sound of it, he repeated it. 'Bah! We are well into the meeting. You may as well get lost now.' Shekhar was only too glad to oblige and promptly vanished from the scene as swiftly as he had appeared.

Pear-shaped Mr Ramesh, the history master, noticing two or three junior teachers hide their smiles as they gave him quick, sidelong glances, self-consciously tried to shrink into his chair. Mr Keshav spontaneously placed his hands over the lower part of his face in an effort to hide his triple chin. Ms Morrin, the maths teacher, whose movements were always slow and calculated, stirred just a little in disapproval. Only the thin and wiry Mr Hiran Hiran, the art master and a health freak who jogged for an hour every day and lived on organic food, a few sports enthusiasts and some newly recruited teachers looked happy. The silence was growing ominous when Mr Hiran broke it with a huge guffaw. Immediately several annoyed voices spoke together.

'What's so funny, Hiran?' asked Mr Keshav mutinously, his hat trick of chins waggling in protest. 'This is absolutely ridiculous! There are enough games and tournaments being played by the students here without our joining in.' This was Mr Jagmohan's private opinion too and he nodded his head in assent in Mr Keshav's direction.

'Disgraceful! That we should spend our time playing instead of teaching! To think such an absurd suggestion should come from the school's trustees!' exclaimed Mr Rohan, the recently appointed physics teacher, his eyes glinting disapprovingly behind his thick glasses. 'As it is, we don't have enough time to complete the syllabus.'

'No, no, Rohan, you're deliberately misunderstanding me,' Mr Jagmohan protested, aghast at the very idea. 'The trustees want you to play in your spare time, not play instead of teach during class hours.'

'All the playing in the world wouldn't have prevented my hernia operation,' Mr Abhijeet, the geography teacher, said in an annoyed tone.

'And I needed an emergency appendectomy,' wailed Ms Philo. She had submitted her medical bills only the previous week and guiltily imagined she was the trigger for this new crisis. 'How would playing have helped discipline the vestigial organ?' She believed in adding minute details to her descriptions.

'And who said we don't play? I twisted my ankle while playing with the Class X boys,' said Mr Ramesh. Everyone knew he was stretching the truth, for he had thoughtlessly strayed into the grounds when a football match was in full swing and immediately collided with a boy who was celebrating his goal. The boy took the history teacher down with him, and the rest of the delirious players arranged themselves like a mountain on top of them in no time. Mr Ramesh had always wondered why players celebrated in this barbaric manner. 'Might not the ones at the bottom die?' he had asked Mr Sunderlal many times. His question had finally been answered. They didn't die; they merely choked and emerged with bruises, aches, pains and sprains, gasping for air.

Ms Sheetal, the plump Hindi teacher who hated the very notion of motion and spent much of her spare time picking her nose, didn't wish to exert herself to protest, but expressed her feelings by digging deeper into her nose. Mr Sunderlal, as sports master, wisely kept silent, while Mr Shyam responded with another sneezing fit.

'Shyam, I think you and I should control our sneezing at the meeting,' said Mr Jagmohan. 'Thankfully the rain has stopped. Anyway, teachers, I've told you about the subject of discussion for the afternoon. You can mull over this and give your point of view. That's the reason for the special meeting. Mr Vijay wants to talk it over with you before any decision is taken.'

'And knowing Mr Vijay, I'm sure he has already decided what to do. He always convenes meetings after making up his mind just to give people the feel of a democratic decision,' said Mr Ramesh rashly.

The others were aghast at this example of insubordination, but Mr Jagmohan, who privately held the same opinion, pretended not to have heard it, only saying, 'I think you'd better go to your classes and engage the students till the afternoon bell goes, or if you'd like some time to discuss this, you may assign them some more work and do so.'

The teachers were amazed that Mr Jagmohan had actually offered them this option and left the room quickly before he could change his mind. Mr Shyam re-entered his class and issued vague instructions to the students to continue reading the chapters till the bell went and not to fool around. 'I'll give you a surprise test on those chapters soon,' he said in order to bring some credence to his words and immediately beat a hasty retreat.

The students smiled and relaxed. Mr Shyam hadn't specified which chapters they were to study, so they thought they could somehow get out of the test. Amar and his friends decided to make their plans for the commemorative match.

'Hey, let's have some fun preparing a proposal for the teachers!' Amar suggested playfully.

'A proposal for the teachers? What do you mean?' asked Thomas. The others also looked puzzled.

'Well, I meant we could write out a proposal for a match between teachers that is similar to our proposal for the commemorative match, but much funnier. Just for some laughs After all, they've been asked to play more games.'

He didn't expect his friends to concur with his idea but they welcomed it with gusto.

'Cool! Let's do it. We'll use a formal style.' Kishore was the most enthusiastic. And the two boys, helped by several tongue-in-cheek suggestions from the others, came up with the two proposals. The proposal for the teachers ran as follows:

Colonel Nadkarni Memorial Limited Overs Cricket Match between the Teachers of Senior School and the Teachers of Junior School

The late Colonel Nadkarni, a benefactor of our school, was a cricket aficionado. To mark six months of his demise, it is proposed that a 15-over cricket match be played between the teachers of the senior school and the teachers of the junior school. Such a match will not only keep our beloved Colonel Nadkarni's memory alive, it will also ensure that the teachers are physically active and fit. Many of the teachers of Green Park are seen to be sluggish in their movements. There is nothing like regular exercise and physical activity to invigorate people and refresh their minds. A healthy mind in a healthy body makes one salubrious, prosperous and sagacious.

A physically active life would help the teachers resist infections (take for example, Mr Shyam's cold that a mere thundershower had brought on) and in the process, also create a healthy respect for sports. Good physical health will, in turn, provide long-standing benefits like making our staff warm, humane, accommodating, well balanced, even-tempered, happy, friendly and more forgiving towards the students. It would broaden their outlook and help them overlook minor and negligible lapses of the students. It would make them understand that every child is the apple of their parents' eye. Punishing children for imaginary offences, being suspicious about their excuses for not doing homework or torturing them through heaps of homework (Ms Morrin), assignments (Mr Rohan), compulsory PowerPoint presentations (Mr Ramesh) unnecessary questions in class (Mr Keshav), surprise tests (Mr Shyam) and far too many exams (all the teachers) is indirectly hurting the sentiments of their parents . . . This, in turn, makes the parents unhappy and unable to put their hearts into their work and ultimately this affects India's GDP.

It is proposed that Mr Sunderlal help the teachers with physical training and supervise cricket practice sessions. The principal will lead by example; he needs to get rid of his pot belly. If all the teachers, male and female, practise hard (e.g. Ms Sheetal would stop picking her nose if she is given catching practice), the best among them could be picked for the final match. But whether a teacher is selected or not, all of them will definitely benefit from the training. And nothing would have pleased Colonel Nadkarni more than to have all the teachers playing or cheering their colleagues at a cricket match. RIP, our beloved Colonel Nadkarni.

-Amar Kishen and Kishore Krishnan. With inputs from the other students of Class VIII A.

Amar read it aloud while Kishore, Eric, Reshmi and Ajay kept the class in splits by performing a dumb charade of the details in the proposal.

'Hey, where's the proposal for our match, the one you are submitting?' asked Arun, after the laughter had died down.

'That's ready too. It's much shorter. Listen me,' he said and everyone grinned. 'Listen me' was Ms Sheetal's favourite expression.

Colonel Nadkarni Memorial Limited Overs Cricket Match between the Green Park Cricket XI and the Rest of Green Park XI

In just a couple of weeks, it will be exactly six months since the demise of our beloved Colonel Nadkarni. As a tribute to his memory, it is proposed that a 15-over cricket match be held between the official Under-15 cricket team of the school and the best team picked from the rest of Green Park.

Since Colonel Nadkarni was devoted to cricket, we believe that only a cricket match would do justice to the keeping of his memory and lend dignity to the occasion.

We request our dear principal, Mr Jagmohan, who was also a close friend of Colonel Nadkarni, to give us permission for the match. More than anyone else, he and Mr Sunderlal will recognize the need for such a commemorative tournament.

We solemnly promise that no classes will be disrupted or lost due to this and all practice sessions will be held only after class hours.

Thanking you in anticipation

The students of Class VIII A

'Super!' said Jayaram. 'All that remains is for Princi to read it and give his approval.'

'Don't know about approval. He might give his reluctant consent if we can get Sunderlal sir to put in a word for us,' said Kiran.

'Anyway, he asked me to place it on the boardroom table, so I'd better do it before the trustees arrive for the meeting.'

'Boardroom table?' Minu sounded sceptical. 'I can't imagine Princi telling you to do that unless he was totally preoccupied with something.'

'Of course he was preoccupied! That's always the right moment to approach him. He named all possible tables, and I'm sure he'll not miss seeing it if it's placed on the boardroom table. Anyway, he's headed there for the meeting. But I don't have an envelope!' Amar looked dismayed. 'Does anyone, by any chance, have a long envelope?'

'Here, take this,' said Reshmi. 'I'd brought my TC in it. You're lucky it isn't wet.'

'Thanks!' He smiled gratefully at her. 'Good you chose to come back today, and even better that you brought your TC in an envelope . . . I'd have brought mine tucked inside a book.'

'That'd be too civilized for you, Butter. You'd have had it all crushed in your trouser pocket,' said Eric.

'Oh no! There goes the bell!' As if someone had taken the finger off the mute button, a sudden blast of noise filled the air as the students ran yelling out of their classes. Amar quickly folded the two proposals separately and holding them and the envelope in one hand, raced out of the classroom, only to crash headlong into Arjun, who was heading a huge body of unruly children galloping along the corridor. Arjun was returning to the class from the sickroom to collect his bag and sneezed on impact.

As the boys clung to each other like long-lost brothers, the proposals and the envelope went flying out of Amar's hand to land under the feet of the boys swarming the corridor. 'Oops!' Amar let go of his friend and ran frantically after the papers shouting at the same time to the boys, 'Hey, hey, guys, don't step on those!' He finally managed to recover the proposals which now had a fair bit of dirt on them, but since they had remained folded the damage wasn't much. The envelope, thankfully, had floated to the wall and rested against it until Amar plucked it from there.

'What's this all about?' asked Arjun. Amar told him briefly about the plan for the commemorative match while placing the correct proposal into the envelope. He placed the envelope high against the wall and wrote, 'For the attention of Mr Jagmohan.' The ink flowed back and the pen refused to write beyond 'attention'. Exasperated, he borrowed a pencil from a passing boy who stood impatiently as Amar wrote the rest of the words in big, bold letters. He then decided to add 'urgent' before 'attention', and had just managed to squeeze in 'urg' when the boy lost patience and snatching the pencil from his hand, ran away.

Spotting Shekhar in the distance, Amar said, 'Hold these a minute, will you, Arjun? I'll check with Shekhar Uncle if there's anyone in the boardroom.'

Left alone, Arjun pulled the proposal out and read it. Then he opened the other paper and glanced at the first few words. 'Ah, a copy,' he told himself. 'But this paper's not as dirty as the other . . . I'll put this in instead.'

Amar returned and Arjun handed the envelope and the paper to him. 'Thanks, Arjun. Shekhar Uncle says no one's in the room. This is my chance. And get well soon. You look like something even the cat won't drag in. Bye!'

The boardroom was out of bounds for the students and Amar felt awestruck and guiltily excited as he opened the door slowly to enter. The room breathed solemnity. There was a long, well-polished wooden table at the centre with elegant chairs all around. Every place was marked by a glass of water that Shekhar had placed there. The peon wasn't taking any chances after having been ticked off by Mr Jagmohan at the staff meeting. Amar believed that Mr Jagmohan would sit at one end of the table, but couldn't figure out which end. Making a guess that it would be the end closer to the door since, as principal, he would be welcoming everyone in, Amar placed the envelope with the proposal there, stuffed the other one into his pocket and vamoosed from the scene.

———

The trustees led by their chairman were ushered into the boardroom by Mr Jagmohan just as the cuckoo inside the cuckoo clock dutifully came out of its tiny door twice to call out the time. Mr Vijay was very keen that the teachers should enter only after the trustees were seated, so Shekhar, who was in attendance, was asked to bring them in. The staff trooped in slowly, in what they believed was a dignified manner. But Mr Vijay interpreted it differently. He was seated on the chair that Amar had believed the principal would take, because he wanted to watch how the teachers walked to their places and took their seats. This position let him view their posture too. The trustees took the chairs next to his and he asked Mr Jagmohan and the other teachers to occupy the rest of the chairs.

He began the meeting after cutting short Mr Jagmohan's welcome with a brusque, 'They know me, there's no need for an introduction. And clearly you have a cold, Jagmohan. The less you speak, the fewer the germs that will get about.' He looked at the head of the school keenly. 'Jagmohan is unwell. And watching you walk to your seats, I'm more than convinced that all of you are in need of physical exercise. You aren't healthy at all, you drag your feet as you walk, you slouch, the mildest exertion is making you breathless . . .' Here he looked pointedly at Mr Sharma, the junior school maths teacher who was a chronic asthmatic.

'. . . it's no wonder you fall sick constantly and need frequent hospitalization. Your medical bills are shocking! I'm sure you're aware that all over the world the importance of recreational sports is gaining recognition because people are increasingly leading sedentary lives. Lifestyle diseases are on the increase, people suffer from diabetes, hypertension and heart attacks at a young age. We have to take preventive measures. I think Green Park School must make sports and physical exercise compulsory for the principal, the teachers and the support staff. Only Shekhar seems to be healthy. Why? Because he moves about running errands all the time. Shekhar, another glass of water, please. And Sunderlal is healthy too. He ought to be, he's the sports teacher. So what do you say?'

The teachers had plenty to say, but chose to maintain a mutinous and cowardly silence. Finally Mr Rohan spoke, his thick glasses gleaming, 'I'm Rohan, the new physics teacher. I think there is already too much emphasis on sports in this school, sir. For the students, I mean,' he added when Mr Vijay stared him into qualifying his remark.

'We're talking about the teachers, Mr Rohan.' At that moment something white lying on the floor caught the chairman's eye. 'Why, what's this?' It was the envelope Amar had put on the table but had fallen down for it had been placed too close to the edge. He picked it up and read, '"For the urg attention of Mr Jagmohan". What's this, Jagmohan?'

Mr Jagmohan groaned. Too late he recalled Amar's appeal and how he had asked him to place the proposal on any table. And of all the tables in the world, that foolish boy had chosen this table! 'Er, I think it is a proposal from the students that Colonel Nadkarni's six month death anniversary be commemorated with a cricket match.'

'Interesting! At least your students love sports.'

'Not wisely but too well,' muttered Ms Philo.

'Why don't you read it?' Mr Vijay passed the paper to the principal who took one look at it and blenched. 'Come on, read, Jagmohan,' he added impatiently. 'Oh, I'm sorry, you have a cold. Narayan, please read it aloud.' He took it from Mr Jagmohan's limp fingers and handed it to Mr Narayan, his right-hand man on the board.

And Mr Narayan read. The teachers listened, shocked. And squirmed in their seats. Their faces grew hot with embarrassment and red with anger as Mr Narayan enunciated every single word slowly, as if enjoying the narration, as indeed he was.

A few teachers who had begun to doze woke up and listened, as shocked as the rest. Nobody could believe what they were hearing. How could the students have dared put forth such an outrageous proposal? Mad! There was a sharp collective intake of breath from several teachers. Mr Keshav spluttered in rage, Ms Sheetal pushed her finger into her nose as deep as it would go, Mr Shyam sneezed in agitation, Ms Morrin actually half rose from her seat while Mr Jagmohan held his tummy in place and glared ferociously at no one in particular. Except for a few junior school teachers and Mr Hiran who, after the initial shock, appeared rather amused, the rest looked very indignant and resentful.

Mr Narayan tried hard not to laugh; this was really entertaining stuff and he was thoroughly enjoying himself. When he came to the end and read, 'By Amar Kishen and Kishore Krishnan. With inputs from the rest of Class VIII A,' the teachers groaned and exchanged knowing glances.

Mr Vijay applauded. 'You have a set of intelligent students. Very well put, the proposal, though, er, there were some unnecessary personal remarks. But truthful, and I appreciate frankness. This is something like a frank feedback with a solution attached. Please congratulate them for me. On second thoughts, I'll do it myself. I've decided to make the announcement at the assembly tomorrow, Jagmohan. I think this is a great idea. Jagmohan, Sunderlal, let's go ahead with it. The boys have outlined every detail. Sunderlal, take care of this please.'

'But, sir,' protested Ms Ambika, the young science teacher in the junior section, 'how can we play cricket wearing sarees?'

'You may wear salwar kameez or whatever you wish, from now on,' the chairman answered rashly. 'Let's change the dress code.'

The lady teachers looked stunned. The junior teachers had been requesting a change in the dress code for a long time, but Mr Vijay wouldn't hear of it. 'No, our teachers must wear the dignified saree,' he had said. And now, on the foolish proposal of an idiotic bunch of students, he had given them the consent. The silver lining made them smile a little.

'So that's it. Make the plans. And let's all be healthy, wealthy and wise or what did that boy write? "Salubrious, prosperous and sagacious." Excellent!'

The meeting came to an end soon after and Mr Jagmohan and the teachers went home, furious with Amar and his friends and quite determined to teach them a lesson.

4

The Teachers Strike Back

The rain had left the ground as soggy as bread pudding gone wrong, but that didn't deter Amar and his friends from plotting to utilize the half holiday for a quick game of cricket. Other cricket-lovers gathered for the same purpose but Mohan, the watchman, heard them making their plans and shooed them off. 'No playing this afternoon, boys! Mr Jagmohan asked me to see that all the students leave the school. ALL! There's an important meeting, you see!'

The boys groaned. 'We should've guessed. We're given a half holiday and then banned from playing. How unsporting is that?' complained Amar.

'Shhh, no using any word with sport in it,' Ajay winked. 'Don't you dare forget!'

'Haha, that's right. How about, how unjust is that?'

'Good enough,' said Kishore, 'but given the context, sadistic would be better.'

'It might shower again, boys. You'd better go home.' Mohan sounded annoyed.

To Mohan's delight a few drops of rain promptly fell and the boys were forced to call it a day. As they wandered leisurely out of the school gates, they shared the news about their proposal for the commemorative cricket match with the other boys. The joyful news quickly spread.

In spite of not having been able to play, Amar returned home as charged up as someone just a few steps away from Everest's peak. He was certain the plan would get the principal's go ahead. He changed out of his uniform, and his muddy trousers with the proposal in the pocket promptly found their way into the washing machine. He spent the rest of the afternoon in his room making plans for the cricket match.

The next morning he stumbled in to breakfast to hear his father read aloud from the paper, 'Daring jewel robbery in town. Jewel Thief caught.'

'What? Caught? What kind of a silly jewel thief is this guy, keeping on getting nabbed like this? If I were a jewel thief, I'd be as slippery as an eel, in my black outfit, hood and mask.'

'Please, Amar, don't add this to your list of ambitions,' said his mother, looking annoyed.

Undeterred, Amar went on, suiting action to words, 'I'd run lightly, jump from building to building and use my sword like Zorro to keep away my pursuers; . . . *clank*, *thrust*, *zhigzhig* . . . oops!' The imaginary trademark sign of Zorro he sketched in the air knocked the chair down and the cup of coffee before him went flying, leaving a brown trail as it took the aerial route to a corner of the dining room.

'I'm so sorry, Ma,' Amar exclaimed, looking remorseful as he brought his masquerade to a close. 'I'll . . .'

'No, no, you will not!' His mother got up with a resigned air to perform the regular morning ritual of clearing a mess. It was too much to hope she would ever get a free morning.

'How well you've demonstrated what an excellent thief you'd make, Amar!' said his father sarcastically. 'Every coffee stain and overturned chair will lead to you. By the way, you'd better be careful; the thief was captured close to your school, but his accomplice has escaped.'

'Wow, really? How exciting! Near our own school! If the assistant is anything like his foolish boss, he'd still be lurking about there.'

'Now don't you think up any hare-brained scheme to find him, Amar,' put in his father, quick to read his thoughts. 'It's school, classes and then home for you. Have your breakfast soon and go. Looks like it's going to be a bright day today.'

That's what Amar thought too—sunshine, clear skies and the prospect of getting the go ahead for the Colonel Nadkarni memorial match. As usual he barely managed to join his class for assembly. Mr Vijay was with Mr Jagmohan on stage as the principal went ahead with the routine stuff. Finally it was time for the announcements. Mr Jagmohan, looking as if an incredibly bitter pill he had swallowed was doing push-ups in his throat, pronounced that the chairman of the board of trustees wished to address the students.

'Good morning, my dear students,' Mr Vijay began. 'Don't worry, I'll be brief. I just wanted to tell the whole school that a wonderful suggestion put forth by Amar Kishen, Kishore Krishnan and the rest of Class VIII A has been accepted by us.' Class VIII A applauded cheerfully. 'I believe they take the lead . . .'

'. . . in every disaster in the school,' Mr Jagmohan muttered grimly under his breath.

'. . . in every unique enterprise at Green Park. They've proposed that the six-month death anniversary of our beloved Colonel Nadkarni be commemorated with a cricket match between the teachers of the senior school and the teachers of the junior school.'

'What?' Amar's eyes popped out and his classmates looked bewildered as a low murmur of surprise rippled among the students. This wasn't what they were expecting.

'It's an excellent idea, and unselfish too, for students rarely think beyond themselves. Our teachers really require the exercise only sports can provide. Yes, the well-worded and . . . er . . . frank proposal was read out aloud to the teachers. I wish to personally congratulate the two boys who took the initiative in this sporting plan. Amar and Kishore, and Eric, the class leader of VIII A, please come forward.'

The three boys went up to the stage in a daze while a low hiss of annoyance and discontent could be heard in the background. Their hands were shaken and backs were patted by Mr Vijay, while Mr Jagmohan darted the mother of all glares at them.

As they returned they heard, as if from a great distance, the rest of what Mr Vijay had to say. 'Since there are only two more weeks for the match, the grounds should be left free for the teachers to practise after class hours. Students may help the teachers by giving them useful suggestions and by serving as fielders when the teachers practise. And there you have it! Teachers teach students in class and students instruct teachers on the cricket grounds. How's that for a perfect give and take policy?' He paused, hoping for loud laughter, but nobody even smiled. The senior students were too dumbfounded to react while the junior boys had stopped listening. Their attention span at the assembly rarely stretched beyond five minutes. 'All right, let's have a generous round of applause, children, for Class VIII A, and you may then go to your classes.'

The word 'applause' penetrated the consciousness of the juniors. Anything that helped them give free expression to their high spirits was welcome and they happily obliged. Satisfied, Mr Vijay left the stage with Mr Jagmohan.

The senior students turned on the three shell-shocked boys as they walked like somnambulists to rejoin their line. 'I thought you said *we* were playing the matches,' hissed Jithin.

'Ha, sucking up to the teachers!' smirked Manas, the bully of VIII B, nicknamed 'The Menace' by his schoolmates. 'Now you can spend your evenings bowling ultra-slow paced deliveries in slooooow motion to them.'

'Shut up, Manas.' Amar ground his teeth in anger and frustration. For the life of him, he couldn't figure out how things had gone wrong.

When the students arrived, Shyam sir was already there, having walked briskly to the classroom. The era of exercising at all times of the day had begun. His nose still looked like a red capsicum but the sneezing appeared to have stopped. 'Come on, don't dawdle, quick march, take your seats quickly.' Arjun halted in his tracks to sneeze. 'Move, Arjun, and don't slouch!'

Arjun, who had just gone past him, responded contrarily by stopping abruptly, bending almost double and thumping his feet vigorously on the floor as an explosive sneezing fit took possession of him. Mr Shyam jumped and leapt to the door like an athletic bear, hurriedly pretending he had reached there to usher everyone in. Once the students had taken their seats, he returned to lean against the table and said, 'A surprise test for you. Nothing unexpected, is it, my surprise tests? Get ready. No protests.' He shot a sharp and telling glance in Amar's direction but Amar was too busy sharing dismayed looks with his friends to even notice.

The test was very tough; nobody knew any answers since they hadn't read the chapters Mr Shyam had asked them to. They exchanged their papers to evaluate, and not one student got pass marks. The bell went off and throwing in a parting shot of, 'And get it signed by both your parents,' Mr Shyam vanished from the class.

'Both our parents? What was that all about?' Thomas wore a long face for his mother was the stricter parent and he had always got away with his low marks by getting his book signed by his father. His father was the manager of a bank and loved nothing better than to put his signature with a flourish on any paper placed before him.

Till the lunch break, every teacher came on the heels of the one just leaving with a never before seen urgency; so the students didn't get any time to discuss the mystery of the wrong proposal. Ms Morrin, waddling with surprising lightness that morning, allotted more homework than usual, while Mr Rohan handed the class various vague assignments.

Mr Keshav, his three chins shaking with indignation, did nothing but ask questions, punishing the ones who answered correctly as well as those who didn't by giving them an extraordinary number of lines to write. To Kishore who had answered to the point, he snapped, 'Write a thousand times . . .' When the boy protested, he added, 'And two thousand times, "I will not answer back".' Amar, bridling at the injustice, spoke out hotly for his friend and Mr Keshav immediately ordered him to write, 'I will not speak up for others whether they are right or wrong.'

'But sir, that sentence is too long! It won't fit into a line.'

'That's your problem,' said Mr Keshav, caressing each of his chins with deep satisfaction. 'And for that protest add another five hundred lines.'

'To?' asked Amar. The teacher hadn't specified any number.

'Infinity,' stated Mr Keshav and left the class, popping back the next moment to add, 'and get your impositions signed.'

'By both our parents, sir, like Shyam sir said?' asked Arjun, to the chagrin of the rest.

The others looked daggers at him, but Mr Keshav smiled sardonically and said, 'Both parents? Good idea! Why not?'

None of the teachers had spoken openly about the proposal, but it was obvious the class was in disgrace. Clearly, the angry teachers had come up with their individual methods of revenge.

Finally, after what seemed the longest forenoon session in school since the beginning of time, as Amar put it, the lunch interval arrived.

'Now, Mr Amar Kishen, it's time for the inquisition. Butterfingers par excellence, the world's leading bungler, ace muffer, chump of the first order and blunderer nonpareil, how did you goof this one up? And make it convincing,' said Kishore, trying to look stern.

'Yes, how did you manage it, you dope?' Ajay asked.

'I really don't know!' Amar wailed. 'I can't understand! True, I dropped everything when I collided with Arjun, but I checked the proposal carefully before putting it into the envelope. I asked Arjun to . . . Arjun!' He turned to Arjun suspiciously. 'Did you exchange the proposals when I went to talk to Shekhar Uncle? I remember asking you to hold them.'

'What proposals, man? The memorial cricket match ones? Yeah, sure, I put the cleaner one in.' Arjun blew his nose loudly like an off-key trumpet and grinned. 'Good I noticed, what? You were going to give such a grimy paper to Princi! Chheeesh!'

Amar groaned and put his head in his hands. 'See, it wasn't my fault.'

'The fault, dear Amar, is not in our Arjuns, but in ourselves, that we are butterfingered,' observed Kishore. 'If you hadn't dropped . . .'

'Enough, Kishore, you don't have to rub it in.' Kiran came to the rescue of his friend, who was looking miserable.

'Yep, what's dropped cannot be undropped,' summed up Eric, shaking his head. 'We'll be in the doghouse for a while, but at least we're in it together.'

Reshmi suddenly giggled. 'I'd have loved to see their faces when the proposal was read out. I really can't remember all we put in, but it must have been quite something.'

'I remember the Princi's pot belly!' said Eric with a laugh.

'Ms Sheetal picking her nose!' gurgled Minu. That had been her contribution.

'And what a lot of healthy advice for the teachers!' As one by one they recollected what was in it, their spirits rose and they became cheerful again. They decided to go to the grounds after class anyway and watch the teachers practise.

'I bet it'll be most entertaining,' said Amar, now back to his old self again.

'But don't you think we should apologize to the teachers?' asked Ajay. 'As Eric said, "What's dropped cannot be undropped," but at least we can let them know that the proposal was written just for fun and not for the public eye.'

'Yes, you're right,' said Amar. 'That's the decent thing to do, I guess. Let's do it after the bell.'

Mr Jagmohan, meanwhile, was having his own problems. He couldn't believe his eyes when, as he walked along the corridor, he encountered two junior school teachers, Ms Sudha and Ms Susan, new recruits, in skirts. 'But . . . but . . . but . . .' he had stammered in protest. 'The dress code was changed to help you play cricket more comfortably. How do you think you're going to play in skirts?'

'These are divided skirts, Mr Jagmohan,' said Ms Sudha, stretching the skirt out like a fan. 'The women's cricket teams of England and Australia used to wear them when they began playing cricket.' She had done her homework.

'But that was in the early days of women's cricket,' Mr Jagmohan objected. 'Now they wear trousers.'

'It's early days for us too, Mr Jagmohan,' she countered. Mr Jagmohan groaned and returned to his room to find Ms Morrin and Ms Philo waiting for him. He frowned in welcome.

'Mr Jagmohan, we don't think we can play cricket,' said Ms Morrin, directly going to the heart of the matter. 'We've never played it before. And no, we aren't going to wear salwar kameez to school; we've got used to wearing sarees and are comfortable in them—we really don't want to wear anything else at work. But of course, we can't play in our sarees.'

Mr Jagmohan's head swam.

'And I've just had my surgery, Mr Jagmohan,' Ms Philo added. 'I don't think I'm allowed to play violent games.'

'Violent? My dear Philo, you exaggerate. Cricket's a gentleman's game.'

'That's just it, sir. It's not a lady's game.'

'Women and their logic!' The principal groaned inwardly. Aloud he said, 'All right, all right, I'll talk to Sunderlal. Anyway, he's been given full charge. But please come to the grounds after the final bell goes.'

Saree, salwar kameez, trousers, skirts! Were these really his problems? Mr Jagmohan felt he was going crazy. He rang the bell. 'Shekhar, ask Mr Sunderlal to come here. At once!' he barked.

'Sunder,' he said as soon as Mr Sunderlal came panting into the room. The PT master had been at the far end of the grounds when Shekhar had told him that he was wanted immediately and he had covered the distance at a pace that would have earned him an approving nod from Usain Bolt. 'Remember what Mr Vijay said? You're in complete charge. You make the programmes, you make the rules, and you take all the decisions. You solve all the problems too. And yes, don't forget to send Mr Vijay the report. You're the sole authority, ha!' The sense of relief that took hold of him as he said this made him smile and he waved Mr Sunderlal away with a belatedly encouraging, 'Mind you, it's a great honour! That's all, Sunder.'

Mr Sunderlal, who thought he had been summoned regarding the repair to the shed's door, looked confused. 'Mr Jagmohan, the latch . . .'

'Ach! Latch? Later, later, I've urgent work to do now,' he said. 'And tell Shekhar I shouldn't be disturbed for half an hour.'

As soon as Mr Sunderlal left, Mr Jagmohan took his flask of tea and poured out a generous cup. Then he put his feet on the table, leant back comfortably on his chair to relax, sipped his tea and soon began to snore.

———

At the bell, the students of VIII A went in a huge group to the staffroom, with the two major culprits, Amar and Kishore, pushed firmly to the front by the others. The teachers, preparing to go down to the grounds, found a crowd of students blocking the door. With their heads hanging a little low, the students spoke in a suitably contrite chorus, 'We're very sorry.'

Amar took over and mumbled, 'Shyam sir, teachers, we know you're very annoyed with us, but truly, it was just a private joke. We wrote a proposal for a match between two teams of students, that's what we wanted . . .'

'And you had a lot of fun writing the proposal for a teachers' match, I suppose,' Mr Keshav interrupted sarcastically.

'Er, yes,' Amar, always honest, confessed. 'But by accident the proposals got mixed up . . .'

'Wait a minute,' said Ms Philo. 'Shall I guess who was responsible for the mix-up?'

'Well, it was me, I mean I,' Amar corrected himself when he felt Kishore's sharp punch in the small of his back.

'Actually he dropped them and I mixed them up,' Arjun owned up with a sniff and a wide grin.

'Of course! Had to be the two of you, who else?' Mr Shyam, who was not their class teacher for nothing, remarked drily. 'All right, boys and girls, I think you've been punished sufficiently for this. Let's put it behind us. We're all going to be healthy people now, thanks to you. Go, now, you're causing a traffic jam.' He smiled.

'Thank you, sirs, teachers,' the students said in another chorus and left, quite relieved at having got that off their chests.

'Decent sort, our Shyam sir,' said Amar to Kiran at the same time that Mr Shyam remarked to his colleagues with a sigh, 'I tell you, that boy! Means well, but can't help causing trouble all the time.'

———

There was quite a crowd on the grounds—the teachers, numbering about forty-five in all, and very many curious students. Mr Sunderlal was already there. Ever since Mr Jagmohan had cleverly passed on to him the complete responsibility of the Good Health Programme, as it had come to be called, the sports teacher's mind had been working on how to go about it and he had soon developed a strategy.

'All right . . . everybody!' he roared to get the attention of his colleagues, clapping his hands for good measure. All the boys standing around applauded with gusto. Looking mildly irritated, he turned to them and asked, 'What are you standing here for? You boys can use the far corner of the grounds for your games.'

'Yaay!' shouted a few and raced away to book their territory, but the rest continued to linger there. They weren't going to miss out on this. Mr Sunderlal decided to ignore them. He cleared his throat and began nervously. He had never done this sort of thing before. Yelling at the boys or shouting out instructions and encouragement was more in his line.

'What Mr Vijay said is, er, very true,' he continued, self-consciously. 'There's, um, nothing like physical exercise to keep oneself fit. Those who keep themselves active are definitely healthier and don't fall sick easily . . .'

Mr Jagmohan interrupted him, 'Very true. As principal, I have to walk all over the school. All that brisk walking keeps me fit.' He pulled his stomach in and demonstrated by walking up and down. He foolishly thought that this ploy would exempt him from having to take part in the programme, but Mr Sunderlal had other plans.

Some boys stifled giggles, Manas hooted with derisive laughter and the sports teacher, struggling to keep his composure, continued. 'And, er, breathing the fresh outdoor air clears your head . . .'

'Achooo!' Mr Shyam's first sneeze of the day made up for the paucity of sneezes earlier. Mr Abhijeet, who had been standing next to him, jumped in alarm, placed his hand over the scar of his recent hernia surgery and hurriedly relocated to the back of the group. His doctor had warned him against contracting any kind of infection. But Mr Shyam responded with three more sneezes, after which, red in the face and redder in his nose, he mumbled, 'Excuse me,' only to find there was no one near him.

'Bless you, bless you, bless you and bless you, sir,' Reshmi shouted from afar.

These interruptions had caused Mr Sunderlal to lose track of what he was saying. He desperately tried to collect his thoughts. 'Um, er, so the outdoors is good for us . . .'

'And we are good for the outdoors,' Amar whispered to Eric but his voice carried.

Mr Sunderlal gave up. Abandoning the introductory speech on the relation between physical activity and general good health that he had thought up as an icebreaker, he said, 'But we don't have to play outdoor games to stay healthy . . .'

'Now you're talking!' Mr Sharma perked up. 'How about carom?' He loved carom.

'No, no, carom, chess, cards and such games can't be played during the hour set apart for games. But table tennis and badminton can. Or even a workout at the gym. Similarly, walking, I mean brisk walking, jogging, running are all alternatives. For we can't have all forty-five of us practising cricket at the same time.'

There was an audible sigh of relief.

'So those of you who wish to opt for a workout at the gym, please come to my right.'

Almost all the teachers moved enthusiastically to that side, Mr Jagmohan reaching first.

'No, no, no,' said Mr Sunderlal, exasperated.

The watching boys again clapped delightedly. Mr Sunderlal shot a pained look at Mr Jagmohan, the architect of his misery, but the principal studiously avoided his gaze and struck up an instant conversation with the nearby Ms Morrin.

'On second thoughts, I think I'll decide who does what. But before that let me find out which of the teachers are interested in playing cricket. Cricket enthusiasts, please come to my left.'

Fourteen teachers, including the two lady teachers in skirts, came dutifully to his left and Mr Sunderlal noticed them for the first time. He frowned. 'Er, Sudha, Susan, why are you wearing skirts?'

'To play cricket. We've already explained to Mr Jagmohan,' said Ms Susan, with a bright smile.

Looking annoyed, Mr Sunderlal turned to Mr Jagmohan who, continuing his policy of not meeting the PT teacher's gaze, had now turned palmist, reading the lines on his right hand studiously. Reshmi and a few boys clapped, Arjun whistled and after putting an end to the applause with an angry glance at the merry offenders, Mr Sunderlal turned again to the teachers. He took a deep breath and decided to be firm right from the start. 'No, I don't think we can allow that. Either salwar kameez or trousers. You can change into them before practice.'

'Ok, fair enough,' said Sudha with a shrug. 'But today?'

'Today, of course, you can remain in your skirts,' he replied with a frown. 'Ridiculous woman, what did she expect?' he thought to himself.

'Fourteen players is too small a number,' he continued, aloud. 'We need at least fifteen from each section. I'll have to choose.'

He divided the teachers of the senior school and those of the junior school into two groups and asked them to stand in a line. And painstakingly he picked thirty, though some protested vehemently at being chosen. He left out the ones who were very senior, or were recovering from illnesses and surgeries. But he selected Mr Shyam; Mr Sunderlal didn't consider a common cold an illness.

'It's almost like lining up prisoners of war,' observed Amar in a low tone to the others, enjoying this immensely. 'You to the kitchen, you to the workshop, you to the hospital, you to the quarry . . .'

Mr Sunderlal asked the boys to fetch the cricket equipment from the shed, but it was Reshmi who ran ahead of the others to do his bidding.

'Sir, the door was open, the latch doesn't fall,' she announced on her return, staggering under the weight of a couple of bats and pads. The others followed with the rest of the cricket gear.

'Yes,' said Mr Sunderlal, looking worried. 'I'd already told Mr Jagmohan about it, but it's been a busy day for him.' He looked questioningly at the principal.

'I'll look into it tomorrow, Sunder,' said Mr Jagmohan with a ferocious glare. He was furious with Mr Sunderlal for including him in the team, but that was the sports master's revenge; after all he had been given full charge.

'Yes, should be careful, there are thieves around— the Jewel Thief, the Sporting Thief,' said Ms Philo.

'Would be wonderful if the Sporting Thief were to steal our cricket equipment,' said Mr Rohan with a laugh. He, too, was very unhappy at having been selected by Mr Sunderlal for cricket. 'All our problems would be solved! No equipment, no cricket, no tournament, haha!'

Mr Sunderlal and the students looked at Mr Rohan in consternation. He must be out of his mind, making such a sacrilegious comment like that, even in jest.

'Let's hope nothing like that happens,' said Mr Sunderlal shortly. 'Mr Jagmohan, we MUST give this problem top priority tomorrow.'

'Yes, yes, of course,' mumbled Mr Jagmohan vaguely. He was already devising schemes to get out of playing cricket.

'The rest may go to the gym and exercise however they want. Johnny is already waiting there.' Johnny was the gym assistant. 'And those who wish to walk or jog around the grounds may do that. Now for some practice.' He turned to the cricketers-in-waiting.

'Yaay, at last!' the students cheered.

5

Teachers at Play

Mr Sunderlal's troubles were not over yet. Once the teams had been selected, everyone wanted to bat except Mr Rohan, who wished to field on the boundary. If Mr Sunderlal had more hair on his head, this would have been the perfect occasion to tear out clumps of it. He had never expected his colleagues to be quite so trying. When sufficiently roused, the PT master was not known to mince words, and had it been the boys who had proved so maddening, he would have given them a huge piece of his mind. But he couldn't resort to similar tactics with his colleagues. So he did the next best thing. He took a deep breath, silently counted to ten and decided to grant their request.

'All right, then, as you wish,' he said gruffly. 'Let's have batting practice today. There's time only for that . . .'

'Sir, sir, sir,' Amar interrupted eagerly. 'Make it a short match; let it be competitive. Maybe three balls to each player unless, of course, he or she gets out? And we'll total the number of runs scored to declare the winners.'

The rest of the students applauded and, surprisingly, so did a few teachers.

'That's a good idea,' Mr Sunderlal replied. He quickly and randomly picked the playing eleven for the rival teams. 'But let's have only one player at the crease. I'll do all the bowling. Senior school team, your turn first and junior school team, you'll field.' He brushed aside all protests and set the field. Mr Rohan returned reluctantly to stand beside his colleagues. But who would be the wicketkeeper? Only Ms Susan volunteered; fortunately her stage whisper to Ms Sudha, 'Any idea what the wicked keeper does? And why is he wicked?' settled the issue.

Mr Sunderlal turned to Arjun, who had been irritating him for some time, hovering nearby and humming a popular song in a high-pitched nasal twang with sniffs and sneezes as the jarring accompaniment. 'Will you?'

'Aw yeahachoo! Sureacheem! Of course I, sniff, sniff, will, sir,' sang Arjun, who, for all his eccentricities, was an excellent wicketkeeper and often stunned the spectators with inspired and game-changing action behind the stumps.

'So sorry, Arjun, I didn't bring your awful gloves,' confessed Reshmi. 'I actually pushed them deeper into the cupboard with a bat. Didn't want to touch them with my bare hands!'

'Thank goodness,' commented Mr Keshav. 'It's bad enough having a sneezing boy for a wicketkeeper. We don't want to get knocked out flat by his stinking gloves too.' Arjun's old, threadbare, reeking gloves were notorious in school lore but their owner considered them lucky and refused to part with them.

Arjun didn't respond. He quietly donned the decent pair of wicketkeeping gloves and pads and waited while Mr Sunderlal, assisted by some of the boys, fixed the stumps and helped Mr Jagmohan pad up. The principal had volunteered to open the batting, wishing to be done with the ordeal as quickly as possible but regretted his decision soon enough when he found all eyes disconcertingly fixed on him as he got ready to face Mr Sunderlal. The rest of his team and the reserve players stood around with the students and watched with amusement his comical struggle to bend forward and hold the bat while his paunch kept getting in the way. He finally managed an awkward stance and grasped the bat gingerly as if it might, at any moment, bite the hand that held it.

Mr Sunderlal measured his run up. He had decided to bowl gentle pace. He was preparing to run in when Amar yelled at the top of his voice, 'Mr Jagmohan, you haven't taken guard!'

'What guard?' Mr Jagmohan, already jittery, yelped, bit his tongue and dropped the bat.

'Hahaha, the Butterfingers Effect!' Reshmi giggled to her friends as Amar went racing to Mr Jagmohan, picked up his bat and said, 'You take guard to know where your stumps are, sir. Very important. Middle stump guard is safest, sir.' He began marking it with his shoes.

'Amar!' shouted Mr Sunderlal, his patience already tested to its limits. 'Stop it! There's no time for all that today. I'll coach them on rules and technique later. Now will you PLEASE STAY AWAY?'

'I know where the stumps are,' Mr Jagmohan growled at Amar. But very soon he didn't, and neither did anyone else for the first ball the principal faced sent them flying in three different directions.

The whole field appealed. 'Out!' said Kishore, the self-declared umpire, raising his finger in a hook-like curve, imitating Billy Bowden, the eccentric New Zealand umpire.

'None for one!' said Ajay, rubbing it in. Mr Jagmohan, embarrassed and annoyed at the same time, ambled off to his room with the pads still on. When this was discovered, wearing the pads was promptly dispensed with.

'At this rate, the bat and ball too will soon be done away with,' whispered Amar to Kiran.

The stumps were put back in place and Mr Shyam went in next. He had just picked up the bat when his cell phone rang. Mr Sunderlal looked annoyed. Students were not allowed mobile phones in school and though he hadn't expressly asked the teachers to switch off their mobiles during practice, he thought it was understood. Mr Shyam sheepishly took the call and in his confusion, put it on loudspeaker mode. 'Where are you? Always late! And don't forget to bring the potatoes and the beetroot!' It was clearly his wife. Mr Shyam cut the call, turning as red as the beetroot he was expected to buy and ignoring the amused sniggers from his colleagues, switched off the phone.

Self-conscious now, he just about managed to keep off all three balls awkwardly but applied a little more force while fending off the third, which therefore went a little distance and he had the presence of mind to take a run. His class, continuing to feel warm towards him, welcomed it with a wild cheer as if it was a six and he was gratified when they gave him a huge ovation as he left the crease.

'One for one,' shouted Eric this time. 'Or is it one for two, sir?'

'No, no, if three balls are faced without getting out, it doesn't count as a wicket.'

Mr Hiran Hiran, who had been waiting so eagerly for his turn that everyone believed he would whack the ball for sixes, defended the first ball. He got a slight touch to the second and Arjun made no mistake. 'One for two, batsman number three!' called out Minu when Mr Hiran left, looking disappointed. The students had decided to take turns to announce the scores and for good measure, Kiran took on the responsibility of writing the detailed scoresheet.

The next batsman, Mr Ramesh, adopted a stance that covered the stumps. The junior team members and the boys protested but Mr Ramesh refused to budge. He lofted the first delivery that went straight to Ms Sudha at cover. She screamed, hid her face with her hands and promptly ran for cover. But Mr Ramesh was so sure he was going to be caught, he didn't even attempt to take a single. 'No run!' said Kishore. Mr Ramesh glared at him.

'Aaah!' The spectators were disappointed. 'Run, Ramesh sir, run!' urged Reshmi.

The second ball got him plumb in front and a huge appeal for leg before went up, but with Reshmi's words ringing in his ears, Mr Ramesh obediently started to run. Arjun collected the ball, ran him out and appealed with a sneeze.

'Out! Run out!' said Kishore. 'Or is it lbw?' He turned to Mr Sunderlal.

'Lbw,' said Mr Sunderlal firmly. He might be a coach now but the hunger for wickets against his name, any which way they might come, remained as strong as ever.

'One for three, batsman number four!' announced Arvind.

Ms Sheetal stopped picking her nose as she came in next and lazily took up the bat. Mr Sunderlal bowled a very slow delivery but she brought down the bat like a battleaxe even as the ball left Mr Sunderlal's hand. The ball landed harmlessly near the stumps and she promptly bent to retrieve it. 'Howzzat! Out, handling the ball!' appealed Arjun and the junior teachers. Kishore raised his finger after looking at Mr Sunderlal for confirmation.

'One for four, batsman number five, or is it batswoman, batslady or batsperson?' asked Thomas.

'Batsman is fine,' Mr Sunderlal said, walking up to his bowling mark. It wasn't the correctness of the terms used that was worrying him but the quality of the batting on display. He realized he had a lot of work ahead of him if he was to train the staff into becoming passable cricket players. 'Didn't they ever play cricket in school or college?' he wondered irritably.

Ms Naaz, the other English teacher, who was big built but very timid, walked shyly to the crease. Another gentle delivery came from the bowler and she hurriedly managed to get the bat hard on the ball as a self-defensive move and heaved it out of harm's way. It went sailing over the boundary.

'SIX!' A huge cheer went up. She grinned, pleased, and sent the next ball straight into the hands of Mr Sharma, fielding at mid off.

'Out!' appealed the fielders and 'Out!' said Kishore.

'Seven for five, batsman number six!' declared Jithin.

Mr Prakash, the other maths teacher, was preparing to face the ball when Arjun's sneeze unsettled him and with a nervous jump, he dropped the bat and moved away only to be clean bowled.

'Sorry, sir,' apologized Arjun after appealing, 'but you're still out.' Kishore confirmed the status.

It was now seven for six, batsman number seven, as Abdul declared. Mr Keshav, who came next, looked warily at Arjun who grinned at him. With steely determination, Mr Keshav got the bat on the first delivery, but miscued it straight to Mr Akash who realized too late that it was coming to him and dropped it.

'Butterfingers!' Amar shouted, thrilled to foist the title on someone else for a change. Mr Keshav managed to get a run each off the next two balls.

'Seven for seven, batsman number seven, no, batsman number six, no eight, no six for seven . . .' Arun faltered, thoroughly confused.

'Nine for six, batsman number eight,' Kiran prompted him.

Mr D'Souza and Mr Rohan both lasted only one ball each and the score was, as Reshmi announced, 'Nine for eight, batsman number ten.'

'Who is the last player?' Mr Sunderlal looked around.

'You, sir,' said Amar and all the students laughed.

Abashed, Mr Sunderlal, who had forgotten he was in the team, said, 'But I'm the one bowling. So maybe someone from among the reserve players could bat in my place?'

None of his teammates would agree to that—they were looking to Mr Sunderlal to add to their pathetic score.

Mr Mathew, the junior school's biology teacher, said he would bowl. And Mr Sunderlal didn't let his team down, smashing all the three balls for huge sixes. Through the loud cheers, Jayaram's voice was heard declaring the final score, 'Twenty-seven for eight, batsman number eleven.'

The junior school team fared much better. Though Ms Susan, Ms Sudha and Mr Akash lasted only a ball each, the others were able to muster a final total of fifty-one, with Mr Ojhas hitting flamboyant boundaries off all the deliveries he faced. They managed to reach twenty-eight and went past the rival team's score when the sixth batsman was at the crease, making it a four-wicket victory, but Mr Sunderlal made sure that all eleven players got a chance to show their batting skills.

'A four-wicket win for the junior school team!' announced Kishore and the victorious team left, basking in their triumph as they were given a generous round of applause both by the onlookers and the vanquished.

'Men of the match, Ojhas sir and Sunderlal sir!' shouted Amar and ran to give the two teachers a flower each that he had hastily plucked from the hibiscus plant nearby.

'Don't be ridiculous, Amar! You know there's a rule against picking flowers!' exclaimed Mr Sunderlal, but with a smile, while Mr Ojhas waved the 'bouquet' joyfully at the cheering crowd.

The students helped put the equipment back into the shed and after closing the door as best as he could, Mr Sunderlal left the place.

Amar spent most of that evening writing the lines his teachers had given him and came down for dinner only after his father yelled out his name so loudly that it almost brought the traffic on the road outside to a halt.

'Where's the fire? What is it, Dad?' asked Amar, bursting into the dining room.

'It's long past supper time, that's what it is,' Mr Kishen snapped. 'Your mother's been calling you down for the last half hour. And I'm leaving tonight on a two-day official trip.'

'Tonight?' Amar looked thoughtful. 'Oh! Sorry, Ma, I had a lot of work to finish for tomorrow. Wow! Chicken curry! Didn't realize I was so hungry!'

He quickly washed his hands and sitting on his chair, pulled it closer to the table by dragging it over the floor, making it screech like chalk on a blackboard.

'Ugh, Amar!' His father closed one ear with his left hand. 'It was so peaceful here till you arrived!'

'But you're the one who called me, Dad,' said Amar irrepressibly, grinning with his mouth full.

'Hmm. I wanted to tell you to take care of your mother when I'm not here.'

'Oh, you don't have to worry. I always do that, don't I, Ma? You know what, Dad, Ma, we're going to have a cricket match between the senior school teachers and the junior school teachers on Colonel Nadkarni's half-year death anniversary. Ha, you should have seen the trial batting today, it was a treat! Who's a stump? Why's the keeper wicked? What's a guard? '

Amar's eyes twinkled, but his father glanced at him shrewdly and remarked, 'But I thought you were planning a match for the students. What happened to that?'

'Oh, that! There was a slight mix-up and it ended with the plan for the teachers' match.' Amar tried to look nonchalant.

'I suppose you were in the thick of that muddle?'

His son pretended not to hear, giving all his attention to the food on his plate that was disappearing at an astonishing rate even as his mother kept serving more.

'Amar, just don't drag me to meet your principal, ok? I can't stand another half an hour of his innumerable "by the ways" and "I'll have you knows" . . . I can put up with anything else, but spare me that.'

'Of course !' Amar quickly left the table to reappear soon after with a sheaf of papers that he thrust into his father's hands. 'Dad, please sign these.'

'Now what's this?' Mr Kishen looked through them.

'You said you can put up with anything else. Isn't it getting late for you, Dad?' Amar asked.

'No, don't worry, I've enough time to find out what you've been up to. Three marks in a chemistry test! Chemistry imposition! And look at this . . . "I will not speak up for others whether they are right or wrong." So what have you done now? And how many times have you written this? It's going on and on. Why didn't you number the lines?'

'Keshav sir said infinity.'

To Amar's surprise, Mr Kishen laughed. 'So you've given a limit to infinity! You must have really provoked him. I'd like to meet this teacher of yours. No, no, on second thoughts, I would rather not!' He hurriedly withdrew his rashly-expressed desire.

The doorbell rang. 'That must be the driver.' Rajeev Kishen quickly signed the impositions and left, flinging a 'Don't get into any more trouble!' over his shoulder.

The moment he left, Amar turned to his mother, who had been silently watching the exchange between father and son with some misgiving. 'Ma, your signature too. The teachers want both parents to sign. I know it's crazy, and really thoughtless of them, giving you this sort of extra work.'

'Hmmph . . .!' His mother muttered something inaudible and scrawled her name, not looking very happy about doing so.

'Thanks, Ma! Great signature! Looks like Zaheer Khan's!' Amar took the papers, hiding his relief with a broad smile.

The next morning, Amar and Kiran reached school earlier than usual, having managed to perform the rare feat of reaching the bus stop before the school bus arrived, and found it in a state of confused excitement. Students of the junior school, who normally believed that every free second was to be used in tearing about the grounds yelling at the top of their voices, now stood in small disorderly groups, completely absorbed in very animated discussions. The senior school boys too were similarly occupied, while a few teachers walked about looking worried. 'What's up?' asked Amar urgently to a passing Class IV boy.

Grinning from ear to ear, the boy rolled his eyes, feigning surprise. 'Don't know? Eeesh! You must be the only ignorant one on this entire planet. The Sporting Thief has stolen our school's cricket equipment! How cool! The Sporting Thief actually came to OUR school! Hooray!'

'What? The Sporting Thief has stolen our school's cricket equipment?' Amar repeated the boy's words, but there was no corresponding elation in his voice. Instead, he looked and felt horrified. Kiran gaped at him open-mouthed. For a few seconds the two friends remained rooted to the spot as the fact sank in, and then they reacted by racing to the scene of the crime. They didn't find Mr Sunderlal; instead, a lot of curious boys stood in front of the shed arguing and pleading with Puneet, the gardener's assistant, who appeared to be guarding the door, sternly preventing any unauthorized entry.

'A bit like locking the stable door after the horse has bolted,' muttered Amar to Kiran as they sprinted to their class to pick up the details.

6

Sensation at Green Park

There was complete mayhem in class. It was like the tower of Babel, with everyone shouting what sounded like gibberish but was actually an excited rendition of individual views about the sensational event. With great effort, Amar and Kiran were able to piece the story together.

Apparently Aman, a Class VI boy, had discovered the theft. He had been playing cops and robbers with his friends and, as the robber, had chosen to hide near the shed. 'A good place,' he had thought and found the inside of the shed, surprisingly left open, an even better place. The significance of it hadn't struck him and he crouched there, holding his breath and holding the door closed from within. But a cheating cop who had flouted the rules by covertly following the robber's movements through one corner of his eye alerted his fellow cops and very quickly the noisy police tracked him to the shed and dragged him out. An ultra-smart cop then discovered the big cupboard that held the cricket gear wide open and empty. It had been burgled.

Delighted that their imaginary game had suddenly become real, the boys ran quickly to seek out Mr Sunderlal, each eager to be the first to break the news to the PT teacher. Finally the jostling crowd found him and babbled on about their discovery so incoherently that it took a little while for Mr Sunderlal to make sense of their words. Mr Sunderlal reacted with shock; his eyes bulged out, his nose twitched in agitation and his jaw dropped in dismay. This was just the response the boys had hoped for and, satisfied, they had left to execute their next mission, which was to spread the news around the school as quickly and as melodramatically as possible.

Their success was absolute. In no time, the whole school had heard about this and loving every minute of their sudden elevation to heroes, the Class VI boys repeated the story that only got more and more fantastic with every narration. The latest version was that everything in the shed, including the shelves in the cupboards, had disappeared. 'Cut, sliced and carted away! All the cupboards,' Aman had been overheard telling a round-eyed, gawking Class V boy, 'were like Old Mother Hubbard's! Yeah! BARE!'

'I just can't believe this!' Amar said to Kiran in dismay. 'Mr Sunderlal must be terribly upset!'

Indeed Mr Sunderlal was, and at that moment was actually in the principal's room, wringing his hands in anguish and repeating over and over again, 'If only the door had been repaired!' When he felt he had driven home the point strongly enough, he muttered, 'And Mohan says Rajan should have been on duty but his dog was sick, so he went off home. How irresponsible! Is a dog more important than sports equipment, I ask you?'

Mohan, the watchman, shared night duty with Rajan, the gardener, who had his new pet dog, Chuhaa, for company. Amar had mischievously suggested this name for the dog and the owner, naturally, had protested at the misnomer—'Chuha? My dog is no mouse!' But Amar had convinced him it was an excellent name with a foreign ring to it. He had solemnly explained that it was short for chihuahua, a special Mexican breed that Rajan's dog resembled, though in truth the gardener's pet was a phenomenally ugly mongrel. Rajan was mad about anything foreign and immediately christened it Chuhaa, with an extra 'a' on the advice of Eric, whose interest at that time had been numerology. He said it would prove lucky for the pet and ensure Chuhaa a bright future. The dog had been sick ever since, while Eric had moved on to the mysteries of palmistry. Eric said he couldn't help the dog because paws couldn't be read.

'For some people, yes,' said Mr Jagmohan, though he was feeling rather guilty. He knew he had been quite casual about the whole matter. He had neither seen to getting the latch repaired nor had he protested when Rajan wanted the night off because Chuhaa was unwell. At the same time, he didn't want to be held totally responsible for what had happened. 'But Sunder, a thief would know how to pick locks. The Sporting Thief has been doing that all along. So I don't think we could have prevented the theft by replacing the latch.' An inspired thought lit up his face. 'Besides . . .'

'Maybe, but should we have made it so easy for him?' Mr Sunderlal interrupted, his distress giving way to annoyance.

'. . . besides,' Mr Jagmohan continued, 'if we had got the latch repaired and the thief had ruined it, we'd have had to start the repairing process all over again. Additional trouble, expense . . .' He stopped to smile, quite pleased with his line of reasoning. But Mr Sunderlal wasn't impressed.

'Mr Jagmohan, such speculation won't take us anywhere. This time, you've got to do something. Call the police please.'

'Police? What's the need to call them?' Mr Jagmohan sounded cross. 'They'll only disrupt the school routine and complicate matters. And when have the police ever managed to crack crimes? They've been after the Sporting Thief for so long and if they haven't found him so far, I don't think they ever will.'

'But Mr Jagmohan, how can you say that?' Mr Sunderlal was shocked. 'We've lost all our cricket gear, our very expensive cricket gear. Don't you remember that we bought really good equipment only a few months back? It's only in movies that the police are so inefficient. You have to get the police involved.'

Mr Jagmohan shook his head in disagreement. 'I don't see why. Anyway, let me ask the other teachers too, Sunder. I'll have a quick word with them in the staffroom before assembly. Come along.' At that moment someone knocked and Mr Jagmohan, who

81

had just reached the door, opened it with a jerk. Amar stumbled in, caught unawares. Class VIII A had decided, after a vigorous discussion, that the police ought to be informed about the theft and Amar had been nominated to convey this to Mr Jagmohan. Amar had immediately raced to the principal's room to do that.

'Sir, you must call the police,' Amar burst out, gathering his wits about him as he recovered his balance. 'The whole school wants you to.' He thought it prudent to extend the opinion of his class to the whole school.

'Get lost, Amar!' Mr Jagmohan roared. 'I don't need your advice. Butting your head in everywhere! Why aren't you at the assembly?'

'The bell hasn't gone, sir,' Amar shouted over his shoulder as he ran away, pleased he had executed what his friends had dared him to do and got away with it lightly too.

Mr Jagmohan now remembered that he had asked Shekhar not to ring the bell till instructed to do so. As he left with Mr Sunderlal, he said crisply to Shekhar, 'Ring the bell after five minutes. After exactly FIVE minutes, don't forget.'

The senior staffroom was also ringing with opinions and assumptions. When Mr Jagmohan and Mr Sunderlal reached there, Mr Rohan's voice was heard declaring loudly, 'If you ask me, it's good riddance to them!' and it took a while for the teachers to realize that the principal was in their midst. They stood up, looking a little sheepish about the hullabaloo they had been making.

Pretending not to have heard Mr Rohan's remark but secretly pleased with it, Mr Jagmohan began abruptly. 'Do you think we should inform the police? Mr Sunderlal believes we should.'

'It's just a petty theft,' said Mr Keshav, taking pains not to look at Mr Sunderlal who was glaring at Mr Rohan. 'And anyway, the police are already looking for the Sporting Thief. It won't serve any additional purpose, bringing them here.'

Most of the teachers agreed, but Mr Hiran took up for Mr Sunderlal. 'I think we should notify the police. This theft might provide them some valuable clue.'

'Ha, valuable clue indeed!' Mr Rohan sneered. He was the only teacher, other than Mr Sunderlal, who had gone to the shed on hearing about the theft. 'What clues do you expect when a horde of self-styled detectives have been walking in and out of that shed touching everything in sight? The ground was still a little soft because of the rainstorm earlier in the week and might have revealed footprints, but by the time someone had the sense to ask Puneet to stand guard, it was way too late. The entrance to the shed looked as if an unruly herd of cattle had wrestled there.' He added hurriedly, 'I'm not faulting you, Sunder, all of us are to be blamed.'

'Well, then, let's now decide on something sensible,' said the sports master, a stubborn expression on his face. 'The police must be called. Who knows, they might still find some clues. And most importantly, unless we make a formal complaint, we will never be able to claim the lost equipment if it is ever recovered.'

'That'd be just great!' muttered Mr Rohan in an undertone to Ms Morrin.

Mr Jagmohan had to agree there was sense in the PT master's words. At that moment the obedient Shekhar rang the bell. 'All right, then, I'll ring up the police after the assembly.'

———

Mr Jagmohan found a noisy, restless school waiting for him when he reached the grounds. The classes stood in disorderly rows. The little boys were busy nudging one another, giggling and constantly looking over their shoulders in the direction of the shed as if the Sporting Thief might pop up any moment, while the older students continued their excited conversation, paying scant heed to Mr Jagmohan's commands over the mike, 'Stop talking! Silence! Attention, all!'

The mike then decided to join forces with the principal and let out such a wail and a shriek that it succeeded where Mr Jagmohan had failed. The students were collectively shocked into silence. It kept up its screeching for a while longer and finally tapered off with a long-drawn-out whistle. Mr Jagmohan quickly conducted the assembly and without mentioning the theft, asked all the students to go to their classes. 'And be quick about it!' he added sternly.

'Sir, the Sporting Thief . . .' a small boy courageously shouted. But Mr Jagmohan was not to be seen. He had unsportingly stolen out.

'What an anticlimax!' commented Ajay as the students dragged their feet to class.

'Smart Princi! Master stroke!' Kishore sounded approving.

'Cheating!' exclaimed a younger voice. The Class VI boys who had been waiting to bask in the glory of their discovery when it was publicly announced felt deflated and refused to budge until Mahesh, the head boy, mimicking Mr Jagmohan, barked, 'Move!' Startled, they obeyed him but with woebegone expressions.

As the VIII A students strolled into class, Reshmi, recollecting something, spun like a top and announced at the top of her voice, 'Hey, guys, you know what? The Sporting Thief's taken Arjun's gloves too! I asked a Class VI boy and he said there was nothing, absolutely nothing, in the cupboard. Poor Arjun will be heartbroken!'

'Ah! Bet then that the thief is somewhere close by, still unconscious,' said Amar as the others hooted with laughter. 'Dear Arjun's gloves are guaranteed to yield immediate results. One whiff of the special aroma and crash! You've been delivered a knockout punch. By the way, where *is* our hero?'

Arjun was absent that day and had he been the kind of person to bother about such things, he wouldn't have been flattered to know his friends had not missed him. But then Arjun lived too much in his own world to be fussy.

'He must be sick,' Kiran observed. 'He wasn't well at all yesterday, sniffing and sneezing more than wicketkeeping. Remember how he sneezed Mr Prakash out?'

The others laughed at the recollection but almost immediately fell silent as Mr Shyam strode purposefully into the classroom.

Lessons kept them busy after that and they were not able to discuss the theft until the third period, which was PT. Going for PT just before lunch break had always been something the class had objected to earlier, but now they were grateful. They rushed to the grounds where Mr Sunderlal was waiting for them. The sports master gave Amar a warm smile in welcome. 'Thanks, Amar! Nice of you to ask the principal to inform the police.'

'Are they being called, sir?' asked Amar, while all the students eagerly crowded around the teacher on hearing the word 'police'.

'Yes, Mr Jagmohan finally decided to do that. I was with him when he dialled the police station. But there are more problems . . . It seems they are short-staffed right now. The diamond robbery is taking up all their attention . . .'

'And their policemen,' Amar interrupted.

'Exactly!' Surprisingly, Mr Sunderlal, who hated anyone interrupting him, actually nodded in agreement. What with Mr Jagmohan treating the theft rather lightly and the general indifference of the other teachers, he was heartened by the concern and keen interest of the students. 'To make matters worse, a minister's visiting the neighbouring town and policemen are required there for security. But the inspector has deputed a policeman, who's on his way to the town, to take charge of this case also and he might look in if he has the time. He could arrive any moment now.'

'Oh, wow!' exclaimed Reshmi. 'Let's look out for him!'

'Yes, why not? ' Mr Sunderlal sounded approving.

The students looked at him in amazement. Was their no-nonsense PT master who would brook no excuse from his students to miss PT actually letting them off? The robbery seemed to have softened him. He added, 'The policeman will be in mufti. If you see him approach, bring him to the principal's room. I'm going there to hand Mr Jagmohan the report I've prepared for the police. But don't all of you crowd near the gate.' And then he left.

'Can't believe this! Mr Sunderlal's actually given us a free period!' exclaimed Eric, removing his glasses and pretending to rub his eyes in amazement.

'And what's mufti? A name? Did Mr Sunderlal say "in mufti" or "with Mufti"?' asked Thomas, looking puzzled.

'Haha, he said "in mufti",' said Kishore, 'which means . . .'

'Plainclothes!' Amar, Ajay, Eric and Jayaram spoke in a chorus. 'We do know the meaning of some words, dear Mr Walking Dictionary,' Amar added.

'But do you know the origin?' Kishore was unruffled. 'The word is of Arabic descent and originally meant . . .'

'What does it matter what it originally meant? What matters is what it means now,' Amar declared. 'The guy's coming in plainclothes because he's on special duty, as security for the minister. As simple as that!'

But Kishore was determined to educate someone, anyone, about mufti. Chuhaa or even a stray cat would have satisfied him, but Thomas was better game and deserved to be singled out for edification; after all he had made the cardinal mistake of asking the question. Kishore caught hold of Thomas's sleeve before he could escape with the others and began holding forth on all he knew about the word, which was plenty. Thomas tried to wriggle free but Kishore's was a firm grip. He had no chance of escape.

The other students reached the gate and hovered there in a noisy group, irritating Mohan, to whom they explained they had been assigned the task of taking the policeman to the principal. 'Reception committee, eh?' Mohan said sarcastically and soon went off to talk to the gardener who had the sick Chuhaa on a leash.

After a little while, most of the students got tired of waiting and wandered off. Only Amar and a few of his friends remained faithfully at the post, but even their patience was wearing thin.

'Where's this stupid policeman gone? Do you think he's lost his way?' remarked Amar irritably. 'Maybe he isn't coming, after all. Let's go play football.'

'What football?' Jayaram, the school's football captain, pulled a face. 'The footballs are in the out-of-bounds shed.'

'Oh yeah. My bad!' Amar looked rueful.

'My bad? Your good that our Kishore didn't hear you say that,' Eric commented. 'He's just finished haranguing Thomas. Here they come! Poor Thomas! He looks as if he's been struck by a lightning bolt.'

'Hey, look!' exclaimed Reshmi, who hadn't taken her eyes off the lane leading to the school. Sighting a man enter it she began a step-by-step commentary: 'Someone's coming up the lane. Enter the dragon . . . slowly, slowly. Yes, looks like our man, the policeman cometh! Now he approaches stealthily, but uncertainly, almost on tiptoe, taking a zigzag route . . . No, he's not drunk, it's because he's trying to avoid the puddles. I tell you, this lane's the worst in the world; day before yesterday's rainwater is still stagnant there . . . Now he wobbles and stops . . . He takes his mobile from his pocket and listens . . . and, oh, he's turning back! Someone must have told him to head to the next town immediately.'

'He can't do that!' Amar sounded agitated as everyone crowded near Reshmi to take a better look. 'That's not cricket!' Impulsively, Amar opened the gate and ran after him, yelling, 'Stop!'

Mohan, returning with Chuhaa on the leash, was shocked to see Amar push the gate open and shoot out like a rocket. Children leaving the premises during school hours was strictly not allowed and it was his responsibility to keep them inside.

'Stop!' He hollered and, shoving the leash into Minu's hand, raced after Amar. Chuhaa pulled free from Minu's gentle grasp and ran off into the lane.

'Stop!' Minu squealed, giving the dog chase and the other students, pleased with something to do, followed her yelling, 'Stop!' in various tones and pitches. Chuhaa, now miraculously revived, made for the policeman's ankles, making him shout in his turn, 'Stop!' as he jumped nimbly about so that the dog wouldn't get a taste of him. The lane, quiet till a few minutes before, was now a scene of lively confusion with everyone's vocabulary reduced to the monosyllabic and arresting word 'Stop!' uttered in various stops.

Amar finally brought some variety into their language saying, 'Chuhaa, go away! Mr Policeman, don't go away. The principal's waiting for you,' he added while Mohan managed to get hold of the dog's collar with one hand and Amar's with the other.

'Policeman?' Mohan sniffed sceptically in the direction of the untidy stranger who had now stopped dancing his diverting jig. 'That? You must be joking! Amar, get back to school.'

Amar pulled himself free with loud protests, 'Mohan Uncle, of course I'm getting back to school; I'm not playing truant! This is the policeman who's come about the theft. We told you we were waiting for him.'

Mohan continued to look disbelieving, so Reshmi clarified, 'He has duty as security for the minister. That's why he's not in uniform but in plainclothes.'

'Mufti, mufti, mufti,' Thomas muttered, determined to use the word whose meaning and origin he had so recently and so painfully learnt. 'He's in mufti,' he repeated, just in case Mohan had missed the point.

Mohan waved the tutoring aside. 'All right then, but get back to school, everyone, and fast!' He held Chuhaa firmly by the leash as the procession returned to school to find Mr Sunderlal and Rajan approach the gates, with Mr Jagmohan slowly walking up. Rajan, after entrusting Chuhaa with Mohan for a while, had gone to get permission from Mr Jagmohan to take him—the dog, not the principal—to the vet and since the policeman hadn't arrived yet, the PT master decided to follow Rajan to the grounds to see whether he had finally put in an appearance. Mr Sunderlal had urged the principal to come along and Mr Jagmohan reluctantly followed.

They had been welcomed with what sounded like a shouting competition that restricted its participants to the use of only the word—'stop'. 'Rajan, Sunder, check what's happening,' Mr Jagmohan gave loud instructions to the other two while he ambled behind. He caught up with them when those who were in the lane had entered the school gates. Before he could remonstrate, Amar hastened to explain, 'Sirs, this is Mr Policeman. We were about to bring him to you.'

'Ah, Chuhaa, you look so much better!' exclaimed Rajan. 'But we'll see the vet anyway. You have an appointment. Come along.' Chuhaa made a futile attempt to renew his acquaintance with the policeman's ankles but Rajan dragged him away.

'My name is Viswas,' said the policeman. 'Constable Viswas.' Mr Jagmohan looked rather disapprovingly at the slight, nondescript-looking man with shoulders that hunched a little, as if trying feebly to show that some of the cares of the police department sat on them. He wore torn, faded blue jeans topped with a crumpled navy blue shirt two sizes too small for him. A dirty cap on his head with its peak turned the other way completed his scruffy appearance. His half-open mouth, which looked as if the firming muscles around it had given up functioning, gave him a goofy, vacuous appearance.

He wasn't in his uniform, but otherwise looked just the sort of idiotic policeman Mr Jagmohan had feared would turn up—the kind of bungler popularized by movies. All that was needed to make the picture complete was a signature mannerism. The principal didn't have to wait long. Rubbing his nose vigorously with his right palm and snorting explosively at the same time, the policeman drew himself to his full height, which was nothing much to begin with anyway, cleared his throat importantly and asked, 'Where is the shed, eh? Take me to it. Quick!' He snorted noisily again.

'Of course,' the Principal replied, a little shortly. He didn't like being ordered about, even by policemen. He was very annoyed with himself for having given in to Mr Sunderlal's implorations and knew the policeman was going to waste a lot of his time. Darting a *I told you so* glance at the PT master, he said, 'Come along. And boys and girls, I don't want you following us. Mr Sunderlal and I will take him around.'

7

Enter Bluebottle

It is not every day that a policeman comes to a school on official duty, and Amar and his friends were quite determined to watch the doings of the constable whom providence had brought to Green Park. Ignoring Mr Jagmohan's orders, they followed the principal, Mr Sunderlal and Constable Viswas to the shed, keeping a safe distance. The constable seemed to be talking non-stop and the effort of listening to him appeared to be telling on Mr Jagmohan, who was looking progressively more irritable. They watched the policeman examine the bolt, the latch and the door by passing his hands all over them.

'Whatever is the guy in plainclothes, I mean, mufti, doing?' asked Thomas.

'Adding to the hundreds of fingerprints already on that door,' said Amar. 'Now they're going in. I bet he'll leave his fingerprints all over the cupboards too. Looks like he's a fingerprint specialist, the kind who specializes in leaving fingerprints everywhere. Think he'll go on all fours with a magnifying glass?'

Mr Jagmohan turned right then and caught sight of the group. The friends immediately tried to look away but he waved to them to come forward. They did so on leaden feet, quite sure they were going to be pulled up. Amar's plan was to pretend it was an unbelievable coincidence—'Oh sir, just imagine, we're all in the vicinity! How extraordinary!' But his theatrics were not required, for the principal actually looked relieved when they reached him. 'Can't you walk faster? I want you to take over and show the constable around. I've got some urgent work in the office. What about you, Sunder?' He offered the lifeline to the PT master who turned it down saying he would like to remain with the policeman.

'In that case, I'll get going. Constable Viswas, here's the report we had made of the theft. And here's my card. Do let us know if, I mean, when, there's news. Thank you!' The principal held his hand out. Constable Viswas, who had just begun to rub his nose with his palm, abandoned that pursuit hastily, drew in his snort and shook the offered hand. Mr Jagmohan left the scene, pleased with his smart exit ploy and surreptitiously wiped his hand with his handkerchief as he walked away.

The students couldn't believe their luck. They went into the shed and watched the constable do exactly what Amar had predicted—he touched the empty cupboard all over, pushed his hand right into the empty shelves, then went to the rest of the cupboards and weighed and considered every item they contained. But he stopped short of going down on all fours to examine the floor, thereby denying complete satisfaction to his audience.

'Aren't you going to examine the floor with your magnifying glass, for clues, I mean?' asked the irrepressible Amar.

'Hrmmf!' The constable rubbed his nose again, gave his trademark snort and raised himself to his full height. 'Making fun of the police, eh? Here, hold this while I look into the shoe rack.' He thrust the report into Amar's hand and Amar promptly dropped it.

'What a clumsy boy! Can't even hold some paper! What's your name? Amar? Butterfingers is what you should be called!' He laughed at his own wit as he picked up the report.

'That's what I am known as,' Amar announced proudly. 'It's my nickname.'

'Oh?' The constable didn't look pleased. 'Ok. Nothing here. Let's examine the grounds.'

They went tramping all over the surroundings and finally it was Minu who discovered the spot where a tiny portion of the wall had come down. Everyone instantly crowded about the place and the constable and most of the boys went in and out through the opening as if it was a kind of game, until Ajay drew Mr Sunderlal's attention to it. Too late, Mr Sunderlal realized that whatever footprints might have been there had already been replaced by fresh ones made by so many pairs of enthusiastic feet. He suddenly felt very depressed. The investigation wasn't going very well, to say the least.

'This is how he entered the school,' pronounced the constable, smacking his lips with deep satisfaction. 'Now all is clear. Finally he stole the cricket gear. Firstly he entered the school this way. Thirdly . . .'

'Secondly,' corrected Eric.

'No, thirdly he opened the shed door after secondly going to the shed and finally that's the way he left the school. But before that, he stole the things,' the policeman said, looking disapprovingly at Eric who had interrupted with 'fourthly'. 'And lastly, I'm hungry and it's lunchtime.' He snorted, rubbed his stomach in slow motion and looked at Mr Sunderlal.

'Right, Constable Viswas, let's have lunch if you've done with looking around,' Mr Sunderlal responded resignedly.

'Oh, yes, there's nothing more, is there?' His mouth opened a little more, as if in anticipation of lunch, making him look even goofier.

'How did the thief know where the shed was? Do you think he had been there earlier and done a . . . recon . . . what's that word, Kishore?' asked Ajay, the self-styled detective in the group.

'Reconnoitre,' Kishore's answer came pat.

'Rubbish! In that case, he'd have taken the things then itself. Mr er, Mr er sir, let's go. Bye, boys, and don't interfere in police matters.' The policeman went away with a grim-faced Mr Sunderlal.

'Fifthly, bye, Constable Viswas,' said Eric, after he was out of earshot.

'What a policeman!' exclaimed Kishore. 'He has shades of Shakespeare's Dogberry.'

'Nonsense, Shakespeare never had a dog called Berry!' said Kiran, looking disbelieving. 'I should know!' Ever since he had presented a paper on Shakespeare's biography in his English class, Kiran considered himself an authority on the Bard's personal life. He couldn't understand why people complained about Shakespeare's life being a mystery and that there was too little known about it. He'd have been delighted with only a quarter of what was public knowledge.

'No, idiot, he didn't. This is a blundering policeman whose name is Dogberry. In *Much Ado About Nothing*.'

'Much ado about nothing all right! What a policeman!' exclaimed Jayaram. 'A ridiculous rozzer!'

'A pathetic peeler!' added Kiran.

'A corny copper!' said Eric. A recent lesson on the functioning of the police force had familiarized them with many slang terms for the policeman.

'A barmy bluebottle, that's what he is, all in blue too,' Amar contributed. 'Bluebottle the Policeman!'

'Cool! Let's call him Bluebottle,' said Reshmi enthusiastically. 'Suits him to a T or, rather, to a B,' she grinned. The bell for the lunch break rang and suddenly realizing they were as hungry as Bluebottle, they raced to the classroom, with nothing but food on their minds.

Lunch was, as usual, a communal affair, with everyone sharing their food. The principle of one man's food being another's poison worked to everyone's satisfaction here. Lunch boxes did the rounds at remarkable speed with some owners ultra-eager to trade hated chapatis, idlis or puris lovingly packed by their mothers for the more exotic fried rice or pasta that some other boxes contained.

Foodies located the fare of their choice purely through their well-honed olfactory skills and tried out fancy combinations. Chronic rice-eaters managed to get weird side dishes to go with their rice or experimented with unusual curries that they smacked their lips over, but would never have touched in their own homes. It was amazing how there was an eager mouth for every item. No food was wasted; often the children were left wishing, like Oliver Twist, for more, and mothers were delighted when empty boxes came back in the evening, prompting them to pack identical, hated lunches the following day.

The lively post-lunch discussion was mostly about the disappearance of the school's cricket equipment, the mysterious exploits of the Sporting Thief and the ineffectual Bluebottle. But the million-dollar question was if the cricket match would now stand cancelled. 'After all, how can you play cricket without the right gear?' Eric asked, and his question set Amar thinking.

'Why ever not?' Amar mused. 'Why not improvise and invent a game that is a lot like cricket, but doesn't need proper cricket gear?' He already felt very guilty about the role he had played in the Colonel Nadkarni commemorative match becoming a contest between the senior and the junior school teachers. He believed he had cheated his schoolmates out of a cricket tournament and wished to make amends.

His face took on the vague, dreamy expression that his friends had come to dread, for it was generally followed by one of his 'brilliant' ideas that invariably got them into hot water. Minu, who was giving a very vivid account of policemen in France, having spent some years in that country, and complementing it with exaggerated gesticulations, noticed a lack of response from Amar. She stopped to look pointedly at him, and then said aloud, 'Look guys, red alert! Butter's got that dopey mind-blowing-idea-brewing-in-my-head look!'

Everyone obediently looked. 'Yep, it's happening, in a second, ah, it happens, enlightenment dawns!' exclaimed Kiran with a laugh as Amar's face began to brighten.

'The glow on his face suggests the moment of epiphany,' added Kishore, giving Amar a slap on his back.

'What's that?' asked Thomas involuntarily and could have bitten his tongue when the words were out, for the nuances of mufti still crowded his mind.

'It means revelation or awakening,' explained Kishore eagerly. 'Epiphany is of Greek origin . . .'

The bell rang and Ajay cut him short, 'Saved by the bell! Keep the rest of your Greek epic nonsense for later or better yet, for never.'

Amar, now bright-eyed, said enthusiastically, 'Guys, listen, this is a supercool idea . . .'

'Best to put it in deep freeze then,' suggested Eric with a wink. 'That would be good for all of us. Here comes Keshav sir! Why are our teachers showing so much zeal these days?' he complained in an undertone to Ajay as he strolled to his seat.

Amar's pleased expression, which was plastered on his face the whole afternoon, irritated his teachers and made them apprehensive. But fortunately it didn't translate into anything disruptive, and they wisely left the boy to his own devices.

'My idea, my idea! Listen!' Amar was eager to voice it when the students ran to the grounds after class.

'My kingdom for an idea!' Kishore responded. 'We're already facing the consequences of your first idea, as are our teachers. Look, they've come down to practise but with what will they play?'

'Ah, the plot thickens!' Ajay smacked his lips. 'Come on, let's not miss anything. Hey, some teachers are actually looking pleased. Mr Rohan, especially.'

A few teachers were indeed looking happy. Amar frowned when he overheard Mr Rohan once again say, 'No cricket gear, no practice, no match. As simple as that.'

But they discovered it wasn't quite as simple as that when Mr Jagmohan and Mr Sunderlal joined them. The principal clapped his hands to secure everyone's attention, which he got when Amar decided to help him by hollering, 'Attention, everyone! Everyone, attention!' so loudly that the principal jumped and dropped the paper he was holding.

'Who told you to do that? And making me drop things too!' He stooped to pick up the paper but his hand wouldn't reach the ground. His next effort was much better, with his audible grunt helping him on his way down. Amar, with misplaced altruism, decided to assist him again. He bent down and in one neat movement, took away the paper just when, with great difficulty, Mr Jagmohan managed to put his hand heavily down to collect it, making him lose his balance. He would have fallen if Mr Sunderlal hadn't stretched out a quick helping hand to break his fall.

Mr Jagmohan was livid as he tottered to a perpendicular stance. 'Get lost, all of you! Who asked you to crowd around here? This is stuff only for my staff.'

'Wow!' exclaimed Kishore as the students backed off. 'How's that for poetry, Jay?'

Amar had taken a quick look at the paper before handing it over to the principal and told the others that it was the printout of an email. 'Probably from Mr Vijay,' he guessed.

He had guessed right. It was Mr Vijay's response to Mr Jagmohan's email informing him about the theft. The principal had asked in the mail.

What should we do?

Mr Vijay's response began quite rudely:

What do you mean, what should we do? Any normal person would call the police and see that everything is done to get back what has been stolen. You must be slipping, Jagmohan, if you don't know this. But if by 'what should we do?' you are asking my advice on the planned

cricket match, I say it must go on. Surely the teachers ought to be able to get hold of bats, balls and the rest of it from somewhere or the other? The whole idea is that they get their much-needed exercise. No question of cancelling it. And I'll be coming to watch. I hope all the teachers are by now engaged in regular physical activity. A healthy mind in a healthy body.
Regards
V

Mr Jagmohan wisely left out the first part of the mail while reading it aloud and some of the teachers groaned when he came to the end. 'What's the point in the cricket stuff getting lost if there's no benefit for us?' Mr Rohan grumbled loudly. The students, standing a distance away and straining to listen to what was being said, heard this.

Amar was very indignant. 'I bet it's Mr Rohan, not the Sporting Thief, who took away the cricket gear,' he said, in his impulsive way.

Minu looked shocked. 'Amar! How can you say such a thing? I mean, you can't accuse a teacher of doing something like this.'

'Why not? Are teachers angels? Didn't you hear him say the other day it would be a good thing if the cricket gear gets lost?'

'Yeah,' Ajay seconded Amar and said, 'I heard him too. Rohan sir must have noticed the broken bit of the wall while returning from the lab. It's visible only from one angle; the huge mango tree hides it from the other side. He must have decided to take it away knowing fully well it would be pinned on the Sporting Thief.'

A heated debate erupted over this with the students divided in their opinion and Amar got so completely involved in proving his point and rebutting the opposition's arguments that he forgot to disclose his idea. The teachers, meanwhile, went through the motions of exercise under Mr Sunderlal's half-hearted supervision. When Mr Jagmohan left, making what he thought was a quiet and discreet exit, the others who had all been watching him equally quietly and discreetly, quickly followed suit and slipped away.

⸺

That evening Kiran, Eric and Ajay went over to Amar's for a sleepover. Amar had asked his mother if they could since his father was away and they had a group project to do. Mrs Kishen was only too happy to have the boys stay the night. The theft at their school was news to her, so at dinner they filled her in with all the details, ending with a highly exaggerated account of Bluebottle's exploits that kept her in splits. Ajay, always health-conscious, ate in moderation and went off to Amar's room after dinner, but Kiran, Eric and Amar stayed glued to the table, doing full justice to the food Mrs Kishen kept piling on their plates.

Stuffed parathas, chilly potatoes, fried rice, prawn noodles, sweet and sour chicken and vegetable koftas were all wolfed down with exclamations of appreciation. Mrs Kishen looked on fondly. They all ended up eating way too much for any single meal. Feeling more like pythons than humans, they got up from the dining table only when Ajay came down looking for them exclaiming, 'What? Still eating? Greedy pigs!'

'Goodnight, Aunty, great meal!' said Kiran and burped in appreciation. Always a burper, he had stopped being apologetic about it ever since his research into Shakespeare's life revealed that burping after a meal was regarded as a sign of satisfaction during Elizabethan times. Now he made it a point of using that gesture of pleasure openly.

'Yeah, lovely!' said Eric, patting his stomach. Amar couldn't make the effort to speak; he merely looked very satisfied.

Ajay helped Mrs Kishen take the spare mattresses to Amar's room and make the beds; the others cleverly excused themselves saying they were too stuffed to help.

'Goodnight, Kiran, Eric, Ajay, Amar,' said Mrs Kishen. 'Don't stay up very late. You have school tomorrow.' She left the room with a sigh, quite certain they were going to be up talking till the wee hours. She knew them too well to believe in the group project story anyway.

'Now to business,' said Amar. 'Let's see how we can spy on Rohan sir and recover the lost bats and stuff. But first, listen to my idea.'

'You mean secondly we'll discuss how we can spy on sir, lastly we'll recover the stolen goods and firstly we'll discuss your splendid idea,' said Eric with a wink.

'Right you are, O Bluebottle!' Amar laughed. 'Anyway, this is my idea. Eric, you said you can't have a match without proper gear. That's when I began thinking that you jolly well can! Why don't we play a cricket match using anything other than regular cricket bats, balls, pads, gloves . . . Talking of gloves, what's happened to Arjun? He didn't come to class today. I wanted to call his place but forgot. I guess it's too late to do that now.'

'Ah, I remembered but forgot to tell you,' said Kiran. 'I called and got his dad who said he is in hospital. He needed to be admitted for he was running a dangerously high temperature and had a very severe throat infection too. "No visitors!" his dad said very firmly.'

'That's too bad, his being ill, I mean,' said Amar. 'Poor Arjun! I could see this coming, what with his getting wet and sneezing like a furnace.'

'"Sighing like a furnace", *As You Like It*,' said Kiran. Shakespeare had made yet another forced entry into his life recently. He had to write the poem 'Seven Ages of Man', an excerpt from the play *As You Like It*, ten times as imposition and could quote it backwards now.

'Whatever,' said Amar, 'but we'll keep the tragic news of the theft of his precious gloves a secret till he's better and can respond with words rather than noises.'

'Or sneezes. Now more about your idea. Sounds interesting,' said Ajay. 'Are you thinking of variations like French cricket or beach cricket?'

'Not exactly,' said Amar, pleased that his idea was not summarily dismissed. 'The variation I'm thinking of is mostly to do with what we can use as bats and balls. Once we decide on that, we can devise rules that aren't too different from cricket proper. The idea is that we play cricket without proper cricket equipment.'

'Like my grandfather's walking stick for a bat?' asked Kiran. 'Or my sister's badminton racquet?'

Everyone came up with suggestions that ranged from the sensible to the bizarre. Amar wrote it all down—plastic or aluminium bats, walking stick or any kind of stick, mosquito bat, racquets, curtain rod, rolled-up newspaper, calendar or magazine, torch, ruler, umbrella, long flutes, clipboards, record books, the hard covers of books . . . the list was endless. They decided that the batsman could choose his bat but there should be some specification when it came to balls. Pads and gloves were optional. Sticks cut from trees or a clipboard could act as stumps.

They decided to frame more specific rules during class the next day and went on to discuss how to find out if Mr Rohan was involved in the disappearance of the cricket gear. Amar came up with another idea. 'Why not get Ironman's help? He goes to Mr Rohan's too. We can ask him to spy for us.'

Ironman was the universal name for Raju, the laundry man who wheeled his cart all over town to press clothes. He had been deaf since birth but was a cheerful chap who was especially chummy with Amar and his friends. He came twice a week to Amar's house to iron clothes and Amar tried his sign language skills on him.

'I know he goes to Mr Rohan's house from mine every Thursday evening. Tomorrow's Thursday. I can ask him to take a quick look around Rohan sir's house and his shed for any stolen goods.'

'And I'd like to see you convey all that through your half-baked sign language,' Kiran challenged him.

'Ah, you come along and watch. I'm an expert.'

'I'm sure Kishore will want to come along too. He thinks he's the expert,' said Eric. 'Anyway, we'll plot this too tomorrow.'

'Tomorrow and tomorrow, and tomorrow, there's too much to be done in our tomorrows,' said Kiran. 'Come, dear children, let's away. To bed now. Out, out, light!'

'Ha ha, you idiot!' laughed the others.

8

Crack It Takes Shape

Mrs Kishen woke the boys up in the morning by first pushing open the door noisily and then drawing the window curtains to let in the light. Neither worked. Eric opened his eyes, looked vacantly about, turned on his side and dozed off again. The others didn't even stir. Mrs Kishen now called out, 'Sleep time over! Wake up, it's getting late!' She shook Amar awake and he woke the others. Kiran discovered he had forgotten to bring his uniform shirt and finally wore one of Amar's, which was both too long and too tight for him. He could hardly breathe when he buttoned it and ended up having almost nothing at breakfast, fearing the buttons would burst. Mrs Kishen could barely hide her amusement as she waved the boys goodbye.

As the boys walked up the lane to their school, they heard someone call out, 'Hello, boys!' They turned to find it was Mr Dinesh Nadkarni, Colonel Nadkarni's nephew and the owner of the colonel's house. He stood at the gate.

'Ah, Mr Dinesh! You're back!' exclaimed Amar, turning so quickly he tripped over his own feet and stumbled.

'Butterfooted too, Amar?' Mr Dinesh remarked with a smile. Amar recovered his balance and laughed self-consciously. He was sure Colonel Nadkarni would have given a great big guffaw in the place of Mr Dinesh's smile. Mr Dinesh was a lot quieter than his uncle and the boys weren't very familiar with him, but they liked him. He occasionally stayed in the house and sometimes also rented it out. 'I've been travelling. I only returned this morning. Town all nice and quiet in my absence, I hope?'

'No, no, Mr Dinesh. Lots of things have been happening, ' Amar explained eagerly.

But the school bell rang at that moment and Mr Dinesh said, 'Really? But there goes your bell! Hurry on. I've thought up a surprise for all of you; I'll be coming to see Mr Jagmohan sometime today and I'll ask him to update me. Bye!'

'Wonder what the surprise is,' panted Kiran, one of his shirt buttons flying off as the boys ran like crazy to reach their classroom, dump their bags and join their class inconspicuously for the assembly. None of them paid the slightest attention to what Mr Jagmohan was saying, going through the motions mechanically as they also tried to whisper to the ones nearby about their innovative cricket match. Mr Jagmohan, after one super glare in their direction, decided to look away for the rest of the assembly. The recent events had already raised his blood pressure and kept it there. He didn't want to allow minor irritants to wreak more havoc to his constitution.

The first period was maths and Ms Morrin, feeling the beginning of a migraine that had come on without any help from the students, gave them some geometry exercises and excused herself to go to the staffroom for her medicine. During that brief period, Ajay addressed the class and quickly told them about the proposed cricket match without using cricket gear. All the students were immediately interested and he asked them to think up details during class. They could finalize the rules during the lunch break.

It was not Ms Morrin but Ms Sheetal, the Hindi teacher, who ambled into the excited class after a while. She was free that period and, finding Ms Morrin looking unwell, had volunteered to babysit the class. With a 'Listen me, do the work Ms Morrin had given you, ok?' she settled comfortably into the chair and spent the rest of the time alternately picking her nose and reading a magazine she had brought along. The students chuckled and, delighted with this bonus time, utilized it in having whispered discussions and jotting down suggestions.

'Plop!' something flew to the table and caught the teacher neatly on her nose, waking her rudely from her sluggish slumber. It was a button from Kiran's shirt, the result of his having taken a deep breath. The class stifled giggles. Ms Sheetal brushed her nose lightly, looked down briefly at the button that now reposed innocently on the table, shrugged and returned to her preoccupations. She later informed Ms Morrin that the class had been absorbed in doing its work studiously and quietly. The maths teacher, however, was not at all convinced by this report.

The next period was English and Ms Philo asked them to write an essay on apartments and their impact on urban life. The students couldn't believe their luck when, instead of walking about as she normally did after giving them an assignment, she sat down to mark some papers. Amar, Kiran and Ajay, seated in one row, continued to make their plans in an undertone. Even when Kiran and Ajay finally began writing their essays, Amar remained busy trying to put the rules together.

Amar realized he hadn't even begun the essay when the teacher asked Eric to collect the books. Thinking quickly, Amar scribbled, 'An apartment or a flat is the most common form of housing these days, what with cities and towns spreading upwards like a giant's long fingernails. A nine-storey apartment building is a very common sight. The roof of the first floor is the floor of the second floor, the roof of the second floor is the floor of the third floor, the roof of the third floor is the floor of the fourth floor and, well, you get the general picture.'

Since Amar's was the last book submitted, it was right on top and Ms Philo opened it as she began lunch. She didn't know whether to be amused or annoyed on reading the essay but the matter was taken out of her hands when Mr Hiran, noticing her expression, picked up the book and passed a casual glance over the composition. His explosive guffaw got everyone's attention and he read it aloud to general amusement. '"The roof of the third floor . . ." the goof!'

'That boy!' exclaimed Mr Keshav, shaking his head. 'Incorrigible. He seemed very busy writing the test, but now I'm not so sure. I think the whole class is again up to something. Let me check his paper. Shyam, just pass that bundle.' The third period had been biology and Mr Keshav, taking a leaf out of Mr Shyam's book, had set the class a surprise test on green, leafy vegetables. Most of the students had utilized the time to think up ideas for the match, beginning to write something only when Mr Keshav said, 'Just ten minutes left.' Amar knew precious little about spinach but what he knew he recorded on paper. He loved to share his knowledge for what it was worth.

Mr Shyam, instead of passing the bundle, located Amar's paper and read aloud, '"Go Green" is today's mantra. Among greens, spinach is one of the healthiest. For proof, read *Popeye* comics, where the hero, Popeye, gets his strength from spinach like Samson got his from his hair and Asterix from the magic potion. Spinach was probably the secret ingredient in the potion Getafix brewed for Asterix. Samson lost his love while Popeye keeps winning his girl, Olive Oyl, back and Asterix wins his battles with the Romans. Moral is that spinach is better than hair for strong, enduring love and victories over enemies . . .' As everyone laughed, Mr Keshav said indignantly, 'That's it? After spending three periods teaching this topic! Ask him something on cricket or any other sport and he spouts details from time immemorial like a free-flowing fountain!'

'Keshav, listen to this. Reshmi's paper,' said Mr Shyam. '"Maybe tomatoes would be a good choice. Not too ripe but ripe enough to burst. Sapota? Good choice again, but not readily available. Kiwi? Unbelievably expensive. Mangoes? Oranges? Apples? A grape is too small and a papaya is too big. No no to potato. A newspaper rolled tight can still send a potato for a six. I'd go for an umbrella . . ."'

'What nonsense is that?' exclaimed Mr Keshav wrathfully. 'Why did that girl have to rejoin the class and add to its madness? Thankfully Arjun's absent. But I asked about greens, not all these vegetables and fruits . . .'

'What is sapota?' Ms Sheetal interrupted, looking curious.

'Sapota or sapodilla is the English name for chikoo,' Mr Keshav explained impatiently. He continued, 'And that Kiran! Is he wearing his baby sister's blouse? He's bursting out of it. A button flew and caught me in the eye when he brought me his answer sheet. My eye's still red. Look!'

'Mark my words,' said Mr Shyam sagely, 'I know my class well. Some madcap scheme is brewing there. Let's wait and see.'

VIII A, meanwhile, had an unusually hurried lunch for they wanted time to get the rules together. Kiran unbuttoned the only button left on his shirt and took great gulps of air in relief before gulping down his lunch. Reshmi took out the paper on which she had jotted down suggestions and was appalled. 'Yikes! I submitted the wrong paper by mistake! Here's my test paper. Oh no! Keshav sir will kill me!'

'Haha, your paper will at least provide some comic relief. He'll need it after reading our answers,' Kishore reassured her. 'Mine will knock him out.'

'All right, everybody!' Ajay said impatiently and clapped his hands to get everyone's attention. 'Hope you've written down the suggestions. Amar will collect the papers.'

Ajay then read them fast, hardly giving anyone time to enjoy the absurdity of most of them. This was followed by a discussion and finally Ajay and Amar retired to a corner to decide on the regulations for the match. Since the two boys had been captains of the school cricket team, nobody objected. Meanwhile, Eric, Kishore and Kiran went to VIII B to sound them on the proposed match. The idea was that the match would be between VIII A and VIII B since classes IX and XI were busy with preparations for the science exhibition. Classes X and XII, with their Board exams, weren't allowed to do anything but study and classes VII and the rest were, according to VIII A, too junior to play a special match. Fortunately this opinion never reached the ears of the 'juniors'.

Eric and the others soon returned with a group of noisy and enthusiastic boys from VIII B, a perennially bored class that welcomed any form of diversion. As soon as they arrived, Ajay read out the rules. 'Welcome, everybody, to the meeting to finalize the rules of a new game that is a variant of cricket. We've decided to call it by a name suggested by Abdul, and that name is "Crack It". Like it?'

A chorus of approval went up and shy Abdul turned red as the others applauded and thumped on their desks while a few slapped his back. Ajay went on, 'The most important feature of the game is that no actual cricket equipment should be used. Bats can be anything except proper wooden cricket bats—sticks, racquets, rolled-up newspaper, whatever. Bats made of plastic or any metal, even gold can be used. Any kind of ball except a cricket ball—tennis, rubber, plastic, table tennis, badminton, soft balls, sock ball, which is a sock with a filling of paper sewed in, balls made of cloth, paper or whatever; in fact, anything round and ball-like can serve as balls, provided the umpire is satisfied with the choice. I hope we can persuade Sunderlal sir to be the umpire.

'The stumps will be sticks or a clipboard. No bails. Helmets, gloves and pads are optional.

'Each side will play five overs. Of the eleven players in each team, one will be the wicketkeeper, five batsmen will face an over each and the remaining five will bowl to the opponents. In other words, five batsmen, five bowlers and a wicketkeeper. The batsman can choose his bat and the bowler will choose the ball he's going to bowl with. Each side starts with 100 runs. If the bat you choose is very narrow you get an additional ten runs. The umpire will determine if the bat qualifies as narrow or not.

'And, this is very important, the fourth ball in every over should be a soft but firm fruit or vegetable. This is the compulsory "Super Ball". There are special rules for this special ball—the batsman has to make sure it doesn't crack open. He shouldn't, er, crack it with his bat. If he does, he is out. Every time a batsman is out, five runs will be taken away from his score . . . But if the batsman negotiates the, er, ball, without cracking it open, he gets six runs. These will be the only sixers. If the ball falls short or falls wide and cracks, five extra runs will be awarded to the batting side. The bowler should strive to be accurate, else his side will concede extra runs. On the other hand, if the ball is accurate but the batsman deliberately takes it on his person or ducks so that the ball bursts elsewhere, he is out. The umpire is the authority to decide if a ball qualifies as the super ball. A too-soft or a rotting fruit will not be allowed.

'Normal cricket rules hold when the other balls are played, except that only four runs are awarded whether the ball crosses the boundary along the ground or takes the aerial route. Field setting is as in the regular cricket matches. The umpire's decision is final in all matters. And since there are negative runs too, the match will end only when the last ball is bowled. That's it. Any comments? Questions?'

'Cool!' exclaimed Jithin, who bowled fast. 'I'm itching to bowl.'

'Will there be a batsman on the other side since every player has to face one full over?' asked Sumay.

'Good question. Yes, someone from his team will be on the other side. And if he gets run out, it is the batsman facing who will be penalized and will have five runs reduced from his score.'

Thomas opened his mouth to ask a question, but Amar, who had been waiting for this, stuffed a hanky rolled into a ball into his mouth and said briskly, 'All your doubts will be cleared in private later, Thomo.'

'Interesting!' said Pranav. 'But there are a few more things we need to know.'

'I know,' Ajay conceded. 'They'll get sorted out when we practise.'

'I'm confused!' Darshil shook his head vigorously. 'All this needs some time to sink in. You'd better put up the rules somewhere. And when, and where, do we practice?'

Manas entered at that moment. 'Ah, therein lies the catch! What's all this I hear about plans for a silly match?'

'It's called Crack It and it isn't silly,' said Eric shortly.

'Crack It? Why not Crack Pot, after the one who came up with this idea? Hahaha!'

'Very funny, Manas,' snapped Amar, scowling. Thankfully the bell put an end to what was promising to become a raging argument and the VIII B boys left.

'What about permission for this?' asked Minu, the conscience-keeper of the class. 'Will Amar . . .?'

'I knew it! It's always got to be me,' Amar, still angry with Manas, muttered under his breath, but the words carried.

'Ah, Butter, cool down!' Kishore put his arm around Amar's shoulders. 'The ideas are always yours and we all know you somehow manage to succeed. The grit, the determination, the diplomacy, the right timing, the magic, the butterfingers . . . you have them all.' He winked.

The next period was history. Mr Ramesh was on leave so it was a free period. The children continued with their discussion so loudly that the teacher in the next class, Mr Keshav, after sending emissaries twice with 'keep quiet or else . . .' messages, finally walked up in person for the 'or else' bit. The class listened to his tirade with great enjoyment. They loved it when he gave them a firing. After exhausting the list of possible future career options for 'noisy, wild, disobedient, unruly, defiant and maddening students' like them that ranged from becoming pirates to becoming restroom attendants, dishwashers and ragpickers, he told them to go to the playground. 'Every one of you! I'll leave the class only after the room's empty.'

9

Dinesh Nadkarni to the Rescue

The students, surprised but delighted, reached the grounds in double quick time. They found VIII B there; it was their PT period. That was even better, for the two classes could now get the details sorted out. Mr Sunderlal wasn't to be seen. Mitra said Mr Dinesh Nadkarni was in the campus and had gone to meet the principal who had soon sent for Mr Sunderlal.

'Ah, so Mr Dinesh's here. Remember he talked about a surprise? He must be sounding Princi about it. Let's go now and ask for permission,' suggested Amar.

'Your sense of timing is indeed deadly, Butter!' Kishore laughed. 'If Mr Dinesh has annoyed him, he's not going to listen to a syllable from you. Still, this looks promising. I'll come with you.'

'Thanks, Kishore.' Amar looked relieved. 'Anyone else coming along? The more the merrier.'

Nobody else volunteered. 'Not in this case, I'm sure,' said Eric. 'We'll come later and pick up the pieces after Princi is done with you, haha. Good luck!'

'Thanks! We'll need it,' Amar replied as the two boys began to walk briskly towards the principal's room.

Coincidentally, Mr Dinesh Nadkarni had also thought of a students' cricket match to commemorate his uncle's six month death anniversary. He had hardly begun to broach it when Mr Jagmohan, after asking Shekhar to bring in Mr Sunderlal, filled the visitor in with all that had happened in the last few days. Mr Sunderlal arrived very quickly and joined in.

Mr Dinesh was astounded. He hadn't heard of the Sporting Thief and was very disappointed to know that the match was to be played only by the teachers. At that moment there was a hesitant knock on the door.

'Come in!' said Mr Jagmohan. Slowly the door opened and Amar and Kishore presented themselves. 'Amar! You again! And Kishore too! If you've come with another mad plan, get lost! I've no time for you and your foolish ideas. Trouble, trouble, trouble, that's all you bring.'

Amar actually began to turn away when Kishore spoke politely but firmly, 'Sir, please, just two minutes. Mr Dinesh, Sunderlal sir, please lend us your ears. This concerns you too. You know we wanted a Colonel Nadkarni commemorative match for the students, but somehow that metamorphosed into one for the teachers. Then the cricket gear got appropriated. The students are very despondent. So we thought we could have an innovative, thumbnail version between the students. We're calling it Crack It; it's a form of cricket without using any proper cricket equipment.'

'What nons . . .' Mr Jagmohan began, but Kishore pretended not to have heard and went on full steam ahead. 'We're sure Colonel Uncle would have been very enthusiastic about it and very supportive too. Actually the match will take less than an hour and can be played on any ground, in which case we don't need to ask for your permission. But since Colonel Uncle was so emotionally attached to Green Park, we thought it would be only fitting to have it here. It need not even affect classes, sir. We can have it after class any evening next week. We require the grounds for just an hour. Please sir . . .'

'Pleeeeeeeease, sir,' added Amar, quite impressed by Kishore's presentation.

'Brilliant plan!' Mr Dinesh Nadkarni smiled approvingly. 'I wanted a commemorative match between students and this is indeed a grand idea! Unique too. Cricket without cricket gear! Why don't you give permission, Mr Jagmohan? I'll take care of the prizes. What do you say, Mr Sunderlal?'

Mr Sunderlal hesitated. He knew such a match had immense scope for disaster, especially if Amar and his friends had planned it. But he too had been feeling sorry for the students and said slowly, 'Hmm, yes, maybe . . .'

'That's it, then.' Mr Dinesh sounded very pleased.

'Give us the details,' said Mr Sunderlal and between the two, Amar and Kishore delineated everything they had planned so far. Kishore also cleverly added that everybody wanted Mr Sunderlal to be the umpire and both Mr Dinesh and Mr Jagmohan eagerly chorused, 'Yes, yes,' while the people's choice grimaced and agreed. It was decided that the match would be held the following Wednesday. The teachers' match had already been fixed for the Monday after that. 'You can give the last period off for the school, Mr Jagmohan,' suggested Mr Dinesh. 'Let all the students watch.'

'Thank you very much, sirs and Mr Dinesh,' the boys said, grinning.

'Wait for me, boys, I'll come with you. Goodbye, Mr Jagmohan, Mr Sunderlal.'

Mr Dinesh left with the boys while Mr Sunderlal stayed behind to remind the principal about the broken wall that had to be repaired. 'Kishore and his "metamorphosed!" "appropriated!" "thumbnail!" Was he taking an "Improve Your Vocabulary" class?' Mr Jagmohan muttered, looking quite displeased while giving a perfunctory ear to Mr Sunderlal's request. It was only after Mr Sunderlal had also left that Mr Jagmohan realized he hadn't actually given the permission. He had been subjected to some gentle but cleverly executed arm-twisting. 'Ah!' he sighed and poured out a cup of tea as a restorative.

The boys accompanied Mr Dinesh on a conducted tour of the scene of crime, taking him to the shed and inside it, and substantiating it with their opinions. As they reached the gap in the wall they saw someone slip furtively in. 'Hey, who's it? Stop!' shouted Amar. The man jumped and caught his shirt on a protruding branch as he turned. It was Bluebottle, in a light blue shirt and without a cap.

'Firstly, what do you mean by frightening me like that?' He glowered at Amar, rubbing his nose vigorously but forgetting to snort. His efforts to free himself led to his shirt getting entangled further and a rending sound followed.

'Secondly, he frightened you and firstly he shouted, Constable Viswas,' said Kishore cheekily, as the boys came to his help. 'Mr Dinesh, this is Bluebottle, er, Constable Viswas, the policeman in charge of the case. Constable Viswas, this is Mr Dinesh who lives in the house adjacent to the school.'

'Oh. Saw anything that night, Mr, er, what did he say your name was?' asked Bluebottle, turning round and round to take a look at the tear in his shirt like a dog chasing its tail and finally giving up when Amar snorted in amusement.

'No, I just got back this morning,' Mr Dinesh replied, hiding a smile.

'Oh, then you're no good.' Bluebottle dismissed him with the snort that was overdue. He turned to Amar. 'YOU don't snort, heard? And why's the wall not closed? Eh? Tell me. I came to see, and what do I see?'

'The wall that's not closed?' Amar responded, grinning.

'Cheeky! These boys are rude. I'll tell the principal.'

'No, no, Constable Viswas, we're very sorry,' Amar apologized, afraid the policeman might throw a spanner in the works. Mr Sunderlal came up at that moment and the boys and Mr Dinesh moved away.

'He is as . . .' Mr Dinesh began when Bluebottle shouted, shaking his fist at them, 'Ass? Don't call me an ass, heard?'

Mr Dinesh looked bewildered. 'When did I call him an ass? What's happening to the police force? What a dope of a policeman!'

'Hahaha,' the boys laughed.

'Dogberry's twin, our Bluebottle, is a prickly chap,' said Kishore. '"Forget not that I am an ass" is what he should have said. That's what Dogberry says in the play.'

After seeing Mr Dinesh off at the gate, the boys returned to tell the others how they had been able to get permission. Now the students of both classes joined in the discussion and plans till the period came to an end. Mr Sunderlal seemed to have disappeared.

'Bluebottle must have knocked him out flat with his snorts,' said Eric.

After school was over, Kiran and Kishore accompanied Amar to his house. They found Ironman pushing his cart away.

'Pfff!' panted Amar. 'Reached in the nick of time. No point shouting. I'll get his attention.' He overtook Raju and turned to grin at him. Raju looked delighted to see the boy. He moved his hands back and forth at lightning speed to communicate something to Amar. Amar also waggled his hands and altered his expressions. From a distance, Kishore interpreted the conversation.

'I think he's saying he's very happy to see Amar. That it's been long and he has missed him. I think Amar's trying to say it's the same with him but what he's actually communicating is that he's just had a heart attack. Ironman looks concerned, Amar laughs. Ironman says grimly it's no laughing matter. Amar's holding his head now. Don't know what he wants to say—that he has a swollen head or the water in his brain is beginning to overflow?'

They quickly caught up with Amar and Kishore offered to tell Raju what they wanted. Amar signalled that Kiran and Kishore were his friends and Raju's face was once again wreathed in smiles. Kishore made signs that they wanted Raju to do something for them.

'What?' Raju held his hands up questioningly and turned to Amar.

Now both boys began to gesticulate to him. They told him in sign language they wanted him to look around Mr Rohan's house as well as the shed for cricket bats, balls, gloves or pads. He should let them know tomorrow. 'Where can we meet you?' Kishore signed. Raju responded by pointing towards Amar's house. He was going there again the next day; Amar's mother wanted sheets and pillow covers to be pressed. 'At five,' he signed, showing five fingers.

'Perfect! We'll come tomorrow and see what he has to say,' said Kiran to the others. 'Off now to our houses to make posters about the match and the rules. But before that, tea. I'm so hungry!'

The next morning most of the students of VIII A reached early and set about fixing the posters on trees, on the walls and on the doors of a few classrooms and the staffroom. The News and Views Board that had stood looking forlorn in a corner of the porch was shifted by Amar and Kiran to a more conspicuous position at the centre. They cleaned it and pinned a colourful poster, prepared by Jayaram, on it.

Crack It!

Crack It is the name
Of this fine new game
Anyone can play it
The feverish and the fit;
But this time it's VIII A and B
Whose combat we will soon see.
For rules go to the big tree
Where they're displayed for free.
Come one and all
And have a ball
At 2.30 on Wednesday
Please don't say 'Nay!'

Thomas had prepared a variation of this poster and Amar took it to Colonel Nadkarni's bust and stuck it at the bottom.

Crack It?

What is the name
Of this exciting new game?
Can anyone play it?
The smart guy and the halfwit?
Where are the rules displayed for free?
Why don't you check the big banyan tree?
Are the teams VIII A and VIII B?
Who will win, can you foresee?
Is it at 2.30 pm on Wednesday?
Wasn't that what I heard them say?
Who do you think will come to see?
You, me and the policeman in mufti?

'Colonel Uncle, we're playing a fun match for you,' Amar said to the bust. 'That question box Thomas made this poster in his style. How you'd have laughed! If only you were here.' He looked solemnly and sadly at the bust before moving away when he heard Ajay shout his name. By that time many students were already standing before the posters, reading and commenting on them. Everyone who read them became interested and wanted to play. Class IX was very indignant at being left out. 'What do you mean, science exhibition? As if we can't spare an hour to spray you with tomatoes!' Jaydeep raved. 'You guys didn't even ask us.'

The junior classes were equally unhappy about only classes VIII A and B playing. 'Not fair! Our class discovered the equipment was missing. So we should be playing,' grumbled Aman.

'What weird logic is that?' asked Reshmi, who overheard him.

But after a little bit of sulking and complaining, the classes that were left out got over it and began to look forward to watching the match. 'I bet it'll be more fun to watch than to play,' said Mahesh, the head boy to Jaydev, his friend.

Manas heard him. 'Sour grapes!' he hooted and smirked.

'Correct!' retorted Mahesh and walked away. He had learnt that the most effective method to discourage bullying was for the victims to agree with whatever taunts the bullies flung at them. 'Never rise to the bait Manas throws at you,' he often advised small boys who came crying and complaining to him. 'Ignore him and other bullies like him,' he always added.

Even the teachers began to show interest in the innovative game. 'I told you they were planning something,' Mr Shyam told Mr Keshav smugly.

That evening nobody seemed to want to go home after class. It was Friday and generally some students stayed back because it was the end of the week, but on that day there was an unusually huge crowd on the grounds. The teachers appeared to have got over their initial inhibitions and were actually enjoying their practice. They had manged a couple of soiled and ancient-looking bats from somewhere and Ms Sudha and Ms Susan had brought along the two cricket balls they had actually purchased.

'It's very nice of you to have bought balls,' said Mr Sunderlal, looking pleased.

'We wouldn't have, if we'd known they would cost so much,' grumbled Ms Sudha.

'Or weigh so much,' complained Ms Susan. 'I can't even hold one, and when I try to throw the ball, it falls behind me. How can I ever strike it? I'm sure my bones will break if the ball hits me. I'd rather play vegetable cricket with the Class VIII students.'

'Vegetable cricket?' Amar heard this and was quite indignant.

While the teachers practised in the main part of the grounds and some boys stayed around to watch, many others gathered at the space allotted to the students and tried to play cricket with all kinds of improvised bats and balls. At 4.30 p.m. Amar decided to go home. This time Eric accompanied him because Kiran and Kishore could not be dragged away from a riveting game with a shoe for a bat and a rolled sock for a ball.

The boys found Ironman busy pressing clothes and Amar tapped him on his shoulder. Ironman turned and grinned widely when he saw who it was. Then he bent down to take something he had hidden on a rack under the cart and presented it to Amar with a flourish. It was a bat.

10

Ironman and the Bat

'A bat?' Amar was flabbergasted. He had only wanted Ironman to find out if there was stolen cricket gear in Mr Rohan's house; he never expected him to bring away the loot. Ironman grinned, pointed to Amar, the bat, into the horizon, the shed in Amar's house and again at Amar. He showed the thumbs-up sign, and gave Amar a playful slap on the back that sent him flying only to collide with Mrs Kishen who was fetching more sheets.

'Oops! Sorry, Ma!' Amar's muffled voice came from inside a sheet that had opened to sit like a tent over him. With help from Eric, he surfaced, gasping, only to dive back in to recover the bat he had dropped. He turned to Raju to thank him in sign language and managed to trip over the sheet. This time he didn't let go of the bat and the momentum took him stumbling forward to reach the house in a few ridiculous leaps with Eric in tow.

Once in the safety of Amar's room, Eric began to laugh. 'So much for yours and Kishore's expert skills in sign language! What I gathered from Ironman's gestures is that he found your bat in sir's shed and got it back for you. He probably thought that's what you'd asked him to do.'

'Nonsense! I specifically . . . oh, forget it!' Amar grimaced. 'But we were right, after all. Rohan sir did take the stuff. So what next?'

'What next, you ass, is how you return stolen goods to the owner.' Eric had been examining the bat. 'Look, this bat isn't ours! There are signatures on it. Let me see . . . Impossible! It says here "The 1983 World Cup Winning Team." Wow, the signatures of the 1983 champions, Kapil Dev and co.! This is a very special bat, Butter. A souvenir. And we've, er, stolen it.'

'Whaaaat?? Sssstolen? You must be joking!'

'No, I'm not! Here!' He thrust the bat under his friend's nose. Amar's eyes popped out and his jaw dropped in amazement as he gawked at the signatures of his heroes.

'Now you look exactly like our Bluebottle; the twin that was lost as a baby,' Eric giggled.

'Very funny!' Amar stuck his tongue at him and turned his attention again to the bat. 'Wow! Eric, do you think this is Kapil's sign? Can't make out the Kapil but I bet that's Dev.'

'That's Sunil Gavaskar!' Eric gleefully identified the legend's autograph.

'Don't you think this could be Srikkanth? K and Srikkanth!?'

'Looks like. But whose is this, Butter? Like four tall people walking in the grass. Think that's an M?'

'Madan Lal!' shouted Amar. 'Yusss! What's this? Sunday? Whose name could be read as Sunday?'

'Sandeep Patil!' Eric looked pleased. 'And this, I guess, is Kirmani, though it looks like Hirwani . . .'

'Hehehe. Where's our man of the series, Mohinder Amarnath? Could this be him? What fancy signatures!

Couldn't they write legibly instead of signing like doctors? I think I'll also create a super signature for myself, a distinctive one that no one can forge.'

'And which you yourself will never be able to imitate,' Eric laughed.

Amar winked. 'Did you know, Eric, that Amarnath framed his famous red handkerchief after getting the signatures of the Indian players on it?'

'Cool! Did Steve Waugh do the same with his red kerchief? I think this is Roger Binny's signature.'

'Then the others have got to be, let me think . . .' He paused and reflected for a bit. 'Yep! Yashpal Sharma, Kirti Azad and Balwinder Sandhu. This, this and this. Yaay! Got them!' Amar cradled the bat lovingly to his chest. The boys never tired of watching the 1983 World Cup final on YouTube. They knew every player and every detail of the match by heart.

'Now to solve the mystery of the mysterious Mr Rohan,' said Eric, looking serious. 'Why would anyone dump such a precious bat in the shed?'

'Yes, even if he hated cricket. But if it hadn't been in the shed but somewhere in the house and Ironman took it from there, wouldn't he, Rohan sir I mean, not Ironman, have missed it? Rohan sir never said anything about it today and he should have if he had discovered its loss and believed it was stolen by the Sporting Thief. And if he, Rohan sir again, is no thief himself, but Mr Rohan, an innocent physics teacher, he should have reported the theft, believing he, that is, the Sporting

Thief, not Rohan sir, had taken it. Doesn't make sense,' Amar rambled, puckering his brows in thought.

Eric's head swam. 'It certainly doesn't. Stop, Butter, please! But one thing's clear. We've got to return this. How, is the question.'

'No point asking Ironman to do it. He might only complicate things further. I'll bring the bat in an old guitar case of Arjun's when I come to your place tomorrow for practice. We'll show the others and then I'll hover about Rohan sir's house and try to put it back.'

'Hmmm,' Eric sounded doubtful.

Mrs Kishen called them down for tea and after tucking into the samosas, cakes and pakoras as if he had been starving for days, Eric left. Amar found the guitar case after some frantic hunting that turned his room upside down. He looked at it, puzzled; he couldn't remember when he had bundled the rexine case into this odd shape and pushed it behind some old textbooks and sports magazines in a cupboard. He straightened it and puffs of dust floated up. Hardly daring to breathe, he dusted it carefully with the uniform shirt he had just changed out of, pinching his nose regularly to stifle the sneezes that threatened to rock the room. He didn't want his mother to ask him a series of uncomfortable questions as only mothers can. He then wet his shirt and wiped the case squeaky clean to make it worthy of the honour of carrying such a precious bat.

The guitar case reminded him of Arjun and he went down to the hall to make a call to Arjun's house. Arjun's mother, who took the call, seemed in a tearing hurry and spoke like an outline story: 'Still in hospital—mild pneumonia—getting better—advised complete rest—NO VISITORS ALLOWED.' She raised her voice as she stressed the last three words and ended with, 'Might be discharged Wednesday.'

'Oh, that's the day of our match! Sad that Arjun's missing all the fun. Do give him our get-well wishes, Aunty. Tell him we all miss him. Goodnight.'

'No visitors allowed, no visitors allowed!' Amar grumbled after hanging up. 'I'm sure he'll only get better, not worse, if we visit him.'

'Not if you visit him, Amar. He might have a relapse,' commented his father, who had returned that evening from his trip and overheard him. 'All well here and at school?' he added and made a hasty exit, not wishing to hear anything to the contrary.

The next morning, Amar decided to take a very roundabout route to Eric's place because he wanted to preen himself with the 'guitar' slung casually over his shoulder, never mind that the case looked rather limp with the bat taking up just a little space at the bottom. The mere act of hoisting the case over his shoulder transformed him in imagination into Russel, the lead singer of his favourite rock band, the Heebee Jeebees. On an impulse he decided to wear clothes that would suit his role and changed into a loose shirt with bold black-and-white checks that flapped about him like the sails of a boat. It had been gifted to his father, who had shuddered and promptly passed it on to his son.

Amar's hair now needed some special attention. There was no gel in the house, so he used some shaving cream to flatten his wild locks and with his hands, directed them with difficulty towards the centre so that they stood upright all along it like a cock's comb. For added affect, he slipped around his neck a chain of chunky, multicoloured beads that belonged to his mother. Thus adorned, he sneaked out of his house, though the maid noticed him and teased him saying, 'Joining the circus?' He ignored her and swaggered all the way to Eric's place, inviting many surprised glances, smiles and sniggers. A group of little children gleefully followed him for some time.

All his friends except Reshmi were waiting impatiently for him at the empty ground nearby where they usually played or practised during weekends and holidays. He was greeted with whistles, groans and hoots of laughter.

'So late! Is it the fancy dress that took you so long? We've been dying to see the bat!' said Ajay, wrenching the guitar case off Amar's shoulder. 'We thought you were late because of a Butter-made disaster at home. Why, you look like a disaster yourself!' He began to unzip the case.

'Hey, careful!' Amar snatched it back from Ajay. 'Wait. I'll show it to each of you. If it's passed around, you guys might drop it.' He took the bat out as if it was a fragile piece of antique china.

'Seriously? Ha, look who's talking! I bet you'll drop it more times showing it around than us if we passed it,' said Ajay, sounding annoyed. But Amar wouldn't let go and took it individually to each person. He was pleased with the oohs and aahs from them and was putting it back into the case when Reshmi arrived and let out a low whistle at the sight of Amar.

'Why are you dressed like this, Amar? And what's that?' she asked, pointing to the case. Minu quickly told her all that had happened at Amar's the previous evening.

'Poor Rohan sir! To think we believed he was the thief!' she remarked. She looked at Amar again and shrieked with laughter.

'We still aren't sure,' said Amar darkly. 'And there's no need to laugh like the Mad Hatter.'

'Oh, come on! Don't tell me you don't know,' said Reshmi, trying to suppress her mirth.

'We don't know what?' asked Amar, sounding cross. 'You're so annoying!'

'Prithee, why dost thou not condescend to share thine superior knowledge?' Kishore requested with mock-Shakespearean politeness.

'Didn't you read today's papers? Sir's absolved of the crime!' Reshmi announced dramatically.

Not surprisingly none of the students had; they had been too busy making balls and looking for possible 'bats' to take for the practice session.

'All right, then! Here goes.' Reshmi cleared her throat. 'Special news bulletin. Headlines. Sporting

Thief in Blazing Form Again. The Sporting Thief is back to his burning tricks and has once again set to flames cricket gear; this time it was audaciously done in broad daylight and discovered only in the evening. A very prominent school of the town, Green Park, regarded one of the best in the world, considering it has supercalifragilisticexpialidocious, in other words, marvellous, students like Reshmi P on its rolls, had recently reported the loss of some sports equipment and it is believed the arson-loving thief burnt it at the garbage dump in the outskirts of the town where some people regularly burn their garbage. Consequently nobody paid any attention to him and he got away with his crime yet again. The silver lining is that the dirty, frayed and stinking gloves of the school cricket team's eccentric wicketkeeper, Arjun, have also been consigned to the flames. With that we come to the end of this special news bulletin. Have a nice day!'

Her report got the desired response—surprise and much laughter. She then added, slowly and deliberately, 'This happened last afternoon, probably about 2 p.m. or thereabouts.'

Her friends caught on. 'Afternoon first period! And Rohan sir was in our class!' Kiran gave a long and low whistle.

'And whatever was our Bluebottle doing?' asked Thomas. 'Isn't he supposed to be detecting? Think he's still in mufti?'

'Oh, Thomo, you'll never get mufti out of your system,' laughed Eric. 'Very bad of Kishore, inflicting permanent damage on you like this. To answer your question, secondly, he was busy snorting, finally he was too full to move after overeating and firstly he was rubbing his nose. Some detective!'

'Poor Rohan sir,' said Amar looking contrite. 'I shouldn't have jumped to conclusions like that.'

'But you always do, Butter. That's so typically you. But why worry? Sir doesn't know we suspected him, so it's fine,' said Kishore airily.

'All right, everybody, we've wasted enough time!' Ajay's no-nonsense voice rang out. 'Let's practice for a while. I managed to bring a tomato and an orange. I'm going to practise with my grandfather's walking stick; I want those ten extra runs. Here it is.'

'Won't he miss it?' asked Minu.

'Only in the evening, when it's time for his walk. What have you guys brought? We must plan our strategy.'

Everyone excitedly brought out their makeshift bats and balls. In their respective homes, mothers were at that moment puzzling over missing vegetables and fruits. Every item thus spirited away was critically examined and commented upon by all except Amar. His overworking conscience was troubling him and he wanted to return the bat as quickly as possible but found it hard to get anyone's attention. 'Guys! Guys! GUYS!' he raised his voice. 'Who'll come with me to Rohan sir's house?'

Only Minu volunteered and the two walked briskly, slackening their pace only when they approached Mr Rohan's gate. They decided to linger around for a bit, wait for the coast to be clear and put the bat back in the shed. Craning their necks this way and that like swans looking for food, they were so absorbed in their task that they jumped out of their skins when a voice said loudly from behind, 'Hello! Hello! What's going on?'

It was Mr Rohan. 'Ah, Amar and Minu! I was wondering what a mobile chessboard was doing in front of my house.'

Amar gave a silly, self-conscious grin.

'Nice hairstyle, Amar.'

Amar gave a sillier grin. Minu chortled.

'I know what you've come for.'

Amar gulped in alarm. 'Something that can be a bat or a ball for your match, right?' Mr Rohan continued.

'Yes!' Amar almost hugged him in relief. 'Yup, yep, yeah!' he said eagerly, making his meaning clear.

'I quite like the game your class has invented. It doesn't hold the kind of danger there is in proper cricket. I used to love cricket until a ball crashed into my eye some years ago, almost blinding me. Even now I have very little vision in my right eye.'

'Oh,' said the two children, trying hard not to stare at his right eye through his thick glasses. Involuntarily Amar closed his right eye and, squinting through the left, blurted out, 'Like Pataudi,' before he could stop himself. But Mr Rohan didn't seem to mind. 'A little like that, though my accident was on the cricket field and I haven't lost my vision completely. No, I don't have a glass eye, if that's what you want to know,' he said with a slight smile, embarrassing them.

'We're sorry, sir, we didn't mean to stare,' said Minu, recovering quickly. 'Is that why you dislike cricket now, sir?'

'Yes. But Mansur Ali Khan was very brave and became the captain even with one eye. I'm a coward. But enough of all that. You can search around the shed and take anything you wish. That's stuff left behind by the owner. He said it's all junk and I could do what I wanted with it. I never got the time to dispose of it. So go ahead and take a look. And good luck for your match. Also, some day when you have a guitar inside that case, you can play for me. Bye!' He laughed and went into his house.

'Thank you, sir!' the children said to his back.

'Phew! So human, after all!' exclaimed Amar. 'So that's why he hates cricket! He may have only one properly working eye, but it's pretty sharp. He noticed there was no guitar in my case. Do you think he'd have guessed there's a bat inside? Come, Minu, let's go to the shed.'

The shed was indeed full of junk. They didn't find anything they wanted except a dusty, old golf umbrella. 'Now where should I put this bat?' Amar looked around.

'Why don't you just keep it? Obviously Ironman got it from this shed and sir said we could take anything we wanted from here.'

'Brilliant, Minu! Why didn't I think of that? The bat's now mine! How the others will envy me! Come, let's go. We'll take this umbrella too. I'm going home now. Ma asked me to get back by noon. We're going out for lunch. And I have to put the bat in a safe place in my room.'

'I'll go back to Eric's and tell the others about this,' said Minu.

Amar handed the umbrella to her. 'Give it to them. It could be used as someone's bat. What fun!'

On Sunday morning, Amar got a call from Eric. 'Got something to show you, hahaha. Come over, quick!' Eric refused to divulge anything further, only going 'hahaha' until, exasperated, Amar banged down the receiver. He had anyway been planning to go early, not having been able to practise at all the previous day, and came down for a quick breakfast wearing his chess shirt again. His father grimaced and sought refuge behind his paper. He need not have bothered because Amar left in double-quick time.

He was the first to reach Eric's house, where his friend was waiting eagerly for him. 'Look!' Eric said, holding out a bat. It was identical to the one Ironman had brought.

'Wow! You've got one too! How?' asked Amar in surprise. As he examined it, Eric said, 'My uncle gave it to me. And guess what? It's a fake.'

'What? Fake?' Amar was shocked.

'Yep. Seems after the World Cup victory a lot of bats with the signatures of players reached the market. That victory is so iconic that such bats are manufactured even today. They're made of some plastic material. So much for your precious souvenir!'

Amar's face fell. "Come to think of it, the bat wasn't heavy, but then we all got carried away by the signatures and didn't notice that. Is it legal to copy signatures like this?' he mused. Then he saw the bright side. 'Hey, Eric, can't we use these bats for our match? They aren't made of wood, so we won't be breaking the rules.'

'Cool! I didn't think of that.'

By this time the others started arriving and the two boys decided to wait for everyone to come before telling them about the bats. Ajay felt the opposing team might protest since they seemed a lot like the regular bats. He suggested that one person from each team could use it and this was accepted.

'Fair enough,' said Eric. 'I'll lend my bat to VIII B. I guess I'll be bowling and won't need to bat. Butter here can use his.'

So that was settled and practice began. The vegetables and fruits that had gone inexplicably missing in the homes of the children made their appearance at practice. Amar took up the golf umbrella to face Kiran and smashed the tomato he was bowled right back on his friend's face, where it burst. 'Yuck!' Kiran made a face as he passed his lips over the juice and threw an over-ripe chikoo at Amar's head. Amar ducked hastily and the chikoo landed on the middle stump, tilting it as the fruit split open.

'Clean bowled, Butterfingers!' his friends yelled.

When the hugely satisfying session ended, the fruits and vegetables had left their traces very conspicuously on the players. Amar looked down ruefully at his black-and-white shirt, which was an interesting blend of colours now and realized, like the others, that there would be a lot of explaining to do when he got back home. As luck would have it, Amar's father had returned early and Amar walked into his house to confront not one but two infuriated parents. Mr Kishen welcomed him with a wrathful 'What the . . .!' while Mrs Kishen resorted to an aghast, 'How the . . .!'

Amar looked down ruefully at the ruins of his shirt and mumbled, 'You never did like this shirt, did you, Dad? Looks awesome now, doesn't it? And Ma, see, vegetable and fruit dyes are really effective. Reshmi says this is a brilliant pattern, but, of course, only a good wash will prove how fast they are, hehe.'

'Since when have you become the spokesperson for the fabric industry, Amar?' asked his father. 'Your mother says she couldn't find any tomatoes for the salad. Now come on, what exactly are you and your friends up to?'

Amar sighed and as he explained, his father's face grew more and more incredulous. 'It's sheer madness. Your principal must be crazy to approve of this . . . this . . . absurd game. What's happening to your school? Crack It, indeed! I'd say stop it.'

'Actually, Dad, Mr Jagmohan didn't approve of it but Mr Dinesh Nadkarni did and persuaded Mr Jagmohan to agree. It's a competition to commemorate Colonel Uncle. So the match must go on.' Amar grinned ingratiatingly and ran up the stairs. Mr Kishen looked at his wife, shaking his head in disbelief.

11

Crack It Fever

It was all about Crack It on Monday. There was something about the game, call it its simplicity, that caught everyone's fancy in a way that surpassed even Amar's optimistic expectations. Well, not quite everyone's. Mr Jagmohan stepped out of his car that morning to be greeted with a ripe tomato that fell with a plop at his feet. This soured his temper immediately but he couldn't nail the culprit, for the 'ball' could have been released from just about anywhere, what with most of the students on the grounds enthusiastically playing their own variations of Crack It. If a bag was the bat then a water bottle was the ball; if a book assumed the properties of a bat, a rolled-up handkerchief, snot and all, was hurled towards it. Mr Jagmohan saw a small boy use his long ruler to hook an eraser that missed his nose by a whisker. He glared at the culprit who unfortunately laughed. An eloquent and satisfying lecture on manners later, the principal escaped to the safety of his room where he smouldered for a while, chastising himself for having given permission for the match.

He appeared on the open-air stage for the assembly with a dark frown on his face and angry thoughts in his head. The air of distracted playfulness that prevailed among the students did nothing to improve his mood.

'Students!' he roared into the mike, which promptly went into its squeal-and-shriek act, taking the sting out of his ferocious address. Steeling himself to keep his temper down as the mike came back, tremulously, to normal, Mr Jagmohan cleared his throat and began again, this time changing the roar to a bark to which the mike, strangely enough, did not take exception. 'Students! May I have your attention, please? Stop whatever you're doing and . . . let the assembly begin!' He sounded like a dignitary declaring an international sports meet open, and Amar sniggered.

With a great effort of will, Mr Jagmohan ignored him and wound up the assembly quickly. He then cleared his throat and said, 'I have something serious to tell you. I know we have this sil . . . er . . . this new game, I forget what it is called, on Wednesday. But that's no reason why the school should get converted into a garbage dump. I will not allow any more of this throwing of rotten vegetables and fruits here in the name of playing cricket. Disgraceful!'

Some creatures have a great sense of timing, and two squabbling crows chose that moment to fly in, squawking noisily and, much to the principal's consternation, dropped an over-ripe, much-pecked mango on his right shoe with such force that the pulp burst all around like playful sunrays. 'What the . . .???' He shooed them off angrily as the students suppressed their laughter. Trying in vain to kick the pulp off his footwear and almost skating a little in the process, he guardedly moved to a mango-free zone and yelled, 'Silence! I hope you heard what I said. Anyone seen fooling around with fruits or vegetables will be punished.' Ignoring the crows that immediately cawed their protest from a nearby tree, he ended his interrupted tirade with his trademark exit command, 'Now go to your classes.'

'So that's it, no super ball practice in school,' said Amar during the lunch break.

'Good, in a way,' said Ajay. 'We need to practise with the other balls. The super ball was taking all our attention. Let's select our team after lunch.'

The scene in the staffroom was different, though. Here the teachers, who normally had their lunches quickly before getting back to work, were actively engaged in a mini game of Crack It with some of the contents of their lunch boxes. A limp triangular sandwich doubled as a bat to a ball that was a hard-boiled egg yolk and divided itself into two right-angled triangles on impact; a chilly played forward defensive to a mustard seed; a late cut by a hard puri caused a malai kofta to disintegrate all over the table; a rolled-up chapati sent a pea sailing out of the window to settle on the unruly mop of an unsuspecting Class III boy, a gulab jamoon pulled to cover was eagerly caught by Mr Shyam and devoured. Students who walked past were taken aback by the unusual sounds that escaped from the room.

In the VIII A classroom, the selection process began immediately after lunch. It was very simple. Vinay, speaking for the boys who preferred the passive exercise of watching to actively doing anything strenuous and stressful, suggested that those who were already in the school team should automatically become part of the Crack It team. 'Vacant spots, if any, may be filled on request,' he added.

His suggestion was accepted and the team was selected. Ajay was unanimously made captain and Amar vice-captain. Ajay, Abdul, Jayaram, Arvind and Amar were to be the batsmen while the players selected to bowl were Kiran, Eric, Kishore, Thomas and Minu, who, not being in the school team, had been the first to vociferously and excitedly volunteer, surprisingly beating Reshmi by a decibel. The vacant slot was that of the wicketkeeper.

'So who would like to be wicketkee . . .?' asked Ajay, knowing fully well who it was going to be, and before he could even complete the sentence, Reshmi screamed, 'Like, it's me!'

Kishore grimaced. 'Three words and two errors! As Princi would say, "Disgraceful!"'

'My bad.' Reshmi winked and then grinned broadly when Ajay accepted her offer, a decision made easy since there was no other contender.

'But we still need a twelfth man and a couple of reserves. Who will they be?'

Pratyush offered to be the twelfth man and Ujjal and Arun agreed to be the reserve players, thus bringing the team selection to a satisfactory end. Ajay went on to discuss strategy.

'Batsmen, choose your bats sensibly, keeping in mind two things—one, you cannot change your bat during the course of your six-ball stay, and two, other than the super ball, the other five deliveries can be bowled by any type of ball, except, of course, the cricket ball. Don't forget that you won't be given a chance to settle down and play out a few deliveries to get used to the ball, the bowler or the pitch. We'll have a short boundary, of course, and the pitch too will be reduced in length. Sunderlal sir will see to all that. The list with the batting order and bowling order will be given to the umpire just before the toss and the order has to be scrupulously followed. The list is top secret, so there's no way in which we can choose a bowler who will be the best choice for a particular batsman. Everything depends on chance. Quick thinking and good reflex action is the need of the hour. Balls can be light, heavy, bouncy, erratic, fast or dead slow. And familiarize yourself with the rules. With only one over to play, whether you're a batsman or a bowler, there's really no time to correct mistakes made. So . . .'

'Don't make any mistakes,' Kishore completed the sentence for him. 'But to err is human, so you'll have to divinely forgive, O Captain, my Captain!'

'Ass!' Ajay laughed. 'All right, guys, when we practise during PT period, our bowlers can try out different kinds of balls and decide which ones work best. We don't know what plans VIII B's making.'

'You can be sure if Manas is playing, he'll be up to some nasty tricks. Since he's a bowler, whoever's facing him has to be on his guard,' warned Minu.

'Yes, forewarned is forearmed. Talking about Manas reminds me, I will go and tell VIII B to get the team list ready. We have to put it up tomorrow.'

'Says who?' asked Amar.

'Sunderlal sir. I had a talk with him in the morning to confirm he'll be the umpire. He looked quite mournful but said yes in the end. He'll talk to the teams this evening.' Saying this, Ajay ran out of class just as the bell rang.

In the evening Sunderlal sir and the two teams discussed the rules all over again while the teachers were busy with their own practice session in the main grounds, all except Mr Rohan and Mr Hiran who came over to watch the preparations for Crack It.

'So what are you wearing?' asked Mr Rohan. 'Surely not your school uniform or cricket whites?'

'Oops, we forgot about that!' exclaimed Ajay. 'Any suggestions, sir?'

'I think some dark colours, like the West Indies' maroon or New Zealand's black, would be ideal. I'm sure you're going to get very dirty. What do you say, Hiran?'

'Well, I suggest they stick to white. Artistically speaking, that'd look better. You might get some masterpieces on your shirts by the end of the match,' Mr Hiran responded with a chuckle.

Though it was playfully suggested, the immense possibilities this had for fun appealed to the Crack

It players and they decided on white outfits. They practised for a while using Vinay's foreign umbrella as a bat. This exercise came to an abrupt end when the owner, who had gone to watch the teachers, returned to find his precious property being subjected to gross abuse. Snatching it indignantly from Jayaram who was poised to use the curved handle to hammer the sock ball into the sky, Vinay promptly went off home in a huff.

———

The next day the teams were put up in the News and Views board. Since it was an informal match, Ajay had written only the first names of the students. A curious crowd immediately gathered to read it:

CRACK IT
Grand Final at the school grounds
Wednesday January 9 at 2.30 p.m.

Teams

VIII A	VIII B
Ajay (captain)–batsman	Pranav (captain)–batsman
Amar (vice-captain) –batsman	Hemant (vice-captain) –batsman
Jayaram–batsman	Sumay–batsman

Abdul–batsman

Arvind–batsman

Reshmi (wicketkeeper)

Kiran–bowler

Kishore–bowler

Thomas–bowler

Eric–bowler

Minu–bowler

Pratyush (twelfth man)

Ujjal (reserve)

Arun (reserve)

Nitin–batsman

Ishaan–batsman

Dipankar (wicketkeeper)

Jithin–bowler

Mitra–bowler

Hitesh–bowler

Milosh–bowler

Manas–bowler

Visudh (twelfth man)

Alex (reserve)

Rohit (reserve)

ALL ARE WELCOME

The school matches were usually open to the public, so Amar had prepared a general invitation. He and Kiran were pasting it in the evening on the wall near the school gate when a loud voice hailed them from behind, 'Ho, boys! What's all this?'

Amar, startled, promptly slid into the gutter running close to the wall, dragging Kiran down with him. Looking up, the boys saw Bluebottle peering down suspiciously at them.

'Blue . . . er . . . Constable Viswas! You gave us a fright!' exclaimed Amar.

'Any luck with the Sporting Thief?' asked Kiran as the boys scrambled out of the gutter.

'Not yet, but I hope to nab him soon.' He watched them fix the notice and read it. 'Hmm! Maybe I'll come.'

'You're welcome, Constable Viswas,' Kiran said politely as they walked away.

'I'd quite forgotten about Bluebottle and the Sporting Thief. Crack It has pushed everything else out of my mind,' Amar said to Kiran as they walked to the bus stop. 'After tomorrow, we can restart our investigation. But till then it is nothing but Crack It for me.'

'And for me,' echoed Kiran.

Wednesday began with a mini disaster. Amar managed to coerce his whites into his already bulging bag and thudded down for breakfast with it and the guitar case slung over his shoulder to find that his mother had chosen that day of all days to prepare chicken for his lunch.

'Chapatis and chicken curry for you today, Amar,' she said with a pleased smile as she placed the lunch box on the dining table. 'Will give you added strength for your match.'

'Is your vegetable-throwing affair today?' asked his father. 'What clothes are you wearing for the game?'

Amar's heart sank. He had hoped nobody would ask this. 'White,' he mumbled.

'White?' His mother sounded dismayed. 'But why? Whose foolish idea is this? Won't it get awfully dirty?'

'Of course it will,' his father said. 'Your dear son will be an artist's delight when he returns.'

'Actually, Dad, you're not far off the mark. It was our art teacher's idea in the first place.' Amar grinned.

His father rolled his eyes and sighed. 'I often wonder what kind of a fool school I've put you in.'

The master changer-of-subjects that he was, Amar immediately opened the lunch box and took a deep sniff. 'Chicken curry, Ma? Mmmm, smells heavenly. But I really won't have the time to enjoy it. Think it will leak?'

'It shouldn't. I had closed the box tight. Why did you open it now? Here, give it to me. I'll close it firmly again.'

'It's all right, Ma. I've done it. Now where do I keep the box?' He looked ruefully at his bag, which threatened to burst any moment.

'Why not the guitar case?' His father suggested. 'It appears to have plenty of space. What's in it? Tomatoes?'

'Good idea. It's my bat, Dad,' Amar explained, his mouth full of puri as he shoved the lunch box in. 'No tomatoes,' he added ruefully. 'Ma says there aren't any left. But anyway, I'm a batsman, so I don't have to worry about the balls. That's the bowlers' headache.'

He quickly finished his breakfast and, lifting his heavy bag to his shoulder, lost his balance and staggered against the table, knocking his plate and glass off it.

'Oops!' He caught the plate expertly but the glass shattered into pieces. 'Catching practice!' He grinned sheepishly at his mother.

'Butter!' Kiran called from the gate.

'There's your friend. Now that you've done your good deed for the day, run,' said his father. 'And good luck.'

'Thanks! Sorry, Ma. Bye!' Amar raced off to join his friend. Kiran had a carry bag with him, that contained the balls he was planning to use.

'Let's take an auto, else the tomatoes might turn into pulp,' said Kiran. 'My mother gave me the fare along with the tomatoes.'

Amar was impressed. 'You mean your mother actually gave you tomatoes for the match? Cool! Mine has either hidden or eaten all of them. I couldn't find a single one in the fridge!'

Mr Jagmohan was so certain the students would be very distracted and excitable that day that he wisely cancelled the assembly. Using the public address system, he declared this, adding that there would be only two short periods in the afternoon and classes would end at 2.15 p.m. in view of the match. 'The junior school students may go home and the senior section is expected to go to the school grounds so that the match can begin at 2.30 sharp. And . . . er . . .' He remembered in the nick of time that he should be saying something about the occasion and racked his brains to remember the name of the game and the classes involved. '. . . this . . . er . . . match, the . . . er . . . Cricket Crackers, is in remembrance of the late Colonel Nadkarni. It has been six months since his sad demise. Let us observe two minutes' silence.'

This took everyone unawares and after very audible requests from the teachers for students to stand up and much shuffling of feet, the school finally fell silent. Mr Jagmohan used that time to rummage through his papers for the invitation Ajay and Pranav had given him. 'You may now be seated,' he said as soon as he found it. 'Crack It, an exciting variation of Clock It, I mean cricket, will be played between teams representing VIII A and VIII B. I wish them all the best. You may go now . . . er . . . you may now sit . . . er the classes may now begin.'

The teachers taking classes in both VIII A and B were rather indulgent that day, turning a blind eye and a deaf ear to the restlessness and whispering that went on all the time, though it was pretty trying. Each teacher welcomed the bell signalling the end of a period.

During the lunch interval, Amar found to his dismay that his lunch box had fallen open and the bat was literally swimming in gravy. 'Oh no! Chicken curry all over the signatures!' he exclaimed and took the bat out. Everyone came crowding around.

'What? Chicken curry?' Kiran and Eric eagerly delved deep into the guitar case and fished out the chicken pieces.

'Don't eat . . .' cautioned Minu, but the deed was done and the two boys were soon smacking their lips and hunting for more pieces. 'You're disgusting.' Minu looked disapproving as she helped Amar clean the bat with some paper from the waste-paper basket. 'The case must be full of germs. Remember it belongs to Arjun. Would not have seen a cleaning tissue or water since it was bought.'

'Now it'll see plenty,' said Arun, taking the case to the tap to wash it out. Amar looked ruefully at the bat, which was now tinted yellow.

'Don't chicken out of playing with it,' laughed Kishore.

'Never mind, Butter,' said Ajay. 'The coating of chicken curry might help the ball race to the boundary. Every little bit helps. Come, share our lunch.'

The bell rang for the afternoon's classes and the students could barely contain their excitement, as the periods seemed to drag until finally the last bell went at 2.15. The school immediately exploded into primitive howls of joy and students began pouring out of their classrooms, emptying them in seconds.

The VIII A team members changed into their whites and, taking their bats, balls and other mysterious bags, sprinted to the grounds, Amar sniffing his bat anxiously as he ran. They went to the 'pavilion', a thatched structure erected at the side of the grounds. The principal and Mr Dinesh Nadkarni were already seated and the teachers were beginning to trickle in. Holding Chuhaa on a leash, Rajan was supervising the arranging of chairs by his two young assistants.

Mr Dinesh greeted the players with a smile and as he got up to shake their hands, the VIII B team arrived.

'All set for the historic match?' he asked, shaking hands with all the players.

The players smiled and a few muttered inane responses. Most of them took quick surreptitious glances at the long table on the side to sneak a peek at the prizes. They saw a tray with medals and a couple of big cardboard boxes. What could they contain? Stifling their curiosity, the players placed their assorted and intriguing Crack It equipment on the ground and waited for Mr Sunderlal to signal the beginning of play.

Amar, not wanting to draw anyone's attention to his curry-soaked bat, took it to an inconspicuous corner of the shed. He had just turned his back to it when a dark shape came out of nowhere and dragged it away. Chuhaa had smelt chicken and pulled himself free from his owner.

'Hey, hey, my bat! Drop it!' yelled Amar, springing after it. Chuhaa, naturally, wouldn't let go and dragged it about, in full view of all. This surfeit of attention was just what Amar had wanted to avoid and cursing his luck, he gave chase to the dog that refused to loosen its hold on the handle and led him a merry dance. A few boys joined Amar. Ajay managed to get hold of the end of the leash, forcibly stopping the dog in its tracks. Rajan freed the bat from its mouth and returned it to Amar, looking very displeased, as if the boys needed to be reported to the SPCA.

Amar examined the bat carefully and found that the handle was beginning to wobble. But it ought to last an over, he thought. He looked up to find the eyes of everyone in the pavilion on him and blushed. 'Is it because of the chicken curry on it that Chuhaa ran away with your bat ?' asked Thomas loudly, answering the question on everyone's minds with his question.

'Probably. Now shut up,' Amar hissed and Mr Sunderlal blew the whistle at the same time, putting Amar out of his misery.

12

It's Crack It Time

The two captains walked out for the toss and gave Mr Sunderlal their lists of the players in the correct batting and bowling order. The PT sir pocketed it and handed Ajay the coin that the VIII A captain tossed high. Pranav called 'Heads', and heads it was. The two captains shook hands after Pranav, taking a keen look at the pitch, decided his team would bat first.

Ajay returned to the pavilion and led his team out to the grounds to the loud cheers of the spectators, with VIII A yelling the loudest. Reshmi had been quite determined to do the right thing as wicketkeeper and a roar of laughter greeted her as she came out with a flamboyant swagger, wearing Minu's mother's kitchen gloves, a peaked cap perched jauntily over her monkey cap and huge pads that had been cut out of soft cardboard and sketched on the outside to look like actual pads. They were fastened to her legs with thick rubber bands. Waving merrily to the spectators, she walked with some difficulty to take her place behind the three sticks of unequal height and width that were to serve as stumps.

Pranav and Sumay now walked to the crease to VIII B's enthusiastic applause. Sumay wore pads made expertly from cardboard and fixed with Velcro tape. He carried a long flute that he twirled like a baton, making

161

it clear, to the dismay of Ajay and co., that he was the batsman. VIII A had decided on Eric, a spinner, as the first bowler, wishing to fool the opposition who would expect a pace bowler to bowl the first over. But clever Pranav judged their thought processes well and had selected Sumay, a fine player of spin, as their opening bat. Pratyush, the twelfth man, immediately raced to Eric with the basket containing the balls he was going to use. Mr Sunderlal examined them and indicated they were all right. Next he took a look at Sumay's bat and signalled ten runs. Immediately Anil and Jaydeep, who were in charge of the scoreboard, added ten runs against the batsman's name and ten to the team's score, which read 110 runs without a single ball yet bowled.

Sumay took guard, quite delighted that Pranav's judgement had been spot on. He now tried hard to identify the ball Eric was planning to bowl with, but the bowler hid the ball well as he walked to the top of his run-up. Eric ran quickly and released a tennis ball that spun into Sumay. The batsman was relieved to see what it was—he had practised quite a bit with a tennis ball. He stylishly got his flute to it and sent it soaring over the boundary. A four was signalled. He again got his bat to the next ball, a very slow delivery, but only managed to edge it to the wicketkeeper's right. Luckily for him, Reshmi couldn't hold on to the catch because her enthusiastic lunge snapped the rubber bands of one pad and she fell over the ball instead of taking the catch. Class VIII A's supporters groaned.

Sumay took a single and quickly turned for another on noticing that Reshmi couldn't locate the ball, which seemed to have disappeared deep into the other pad. Reshmi's frantic efforts to prise it out only helped to trap it firmly between the two rubber bands. Another run was taken before she managed to rescue it. That was the end of the pads. She signalled to Pratyush who took them away. Sumay returned to face the third ball, a deceptively slow delivery that pitched outside the off stump, but he waited, got the flute on it and guided it expertly along the ground to the boundary. Everyone applauded the shot, a brilliant one even if it had been played with a regular bat.

The fourth was the super ball. 'Super ball,' announced Mr Sunderlal. Immediately there was a ripple of excitement among the spectators. 'Mango!' yelled a voice. 'Orange!' shouted another. 'Tomato!' a group chorused and as Eric began to walk to the bowling mark, chanted, 'To-mato! Tom-ato! Tomat-ooooo!' But Eric's choice was actually a ripe chikoo and he bowled it straight. Sumay saw it come faster than he had expected and ducked instinctively. Reshmi, who loved chikoos, was delighted to get it on her right shoulder, where it burst. Picking whatever she could off her shirt and eating it, skin and all, was the work of a moment as, smacking her lips, she appealed along with the rest of the fielders. 'Out!' Mr Sunderlal's finger went up and five runs were reduced from Sumay's and the team's total.

Sumay now waited calmly for another slow one. But this time Eric bowled fast, catching the batsman off guard and sending the stumps flying. The last delivery was straight and Sumay managed to flick it for a quick single. Mahesh, the head boy, and Jaydev were also keeping scores and when Sumay's innings came to an end, the two boys announced, 'Sumay twelve runs and VIII B 112.' Nobody had asked them to do that, but everyone immediately checked the scoreboard and when they saw that it tallied with the score announced, applauded. Pleased, the boys decided to continue making announcements about the score and no one stopped them.

Sumay walked to the other end when Pranav, the number two bat, went to the pavilion to pick up his bat, the one Eric had given him, and returned to the crease where he put on the pads left there by Sumay. Pratyush brought Minu, bowler number two, the basket with the balls and took back Eric's.

Minu had chosen a plastic ball. Unfortunately a light wind began to blow against her and the first ball stopped halfway down the pitch. Two runs were the penalty for such a ball, which wouldn't be counted as a no ball, though, and were added to VIII B's score as extras. The second and third balls only reached a little further. Four more extras and the bowler looked miserable. But so did the batsman, for Pranav had been hoping to score a lot of runs with a bat that was the closest to a regular one. The super ball was a ripe orange. 'Orange,' said Mr Sunderlal. 'Orange,' shouted Jaydev. 'Orange!!' echoed all the students. Minu's delivery was right on target. Pranav got a touch to it and it burst. 'Orange juice!' yelled Prahlad as Mr Sunderlal signalled for five runs to be taken away.

Minu perked up. The wind was still now and the next ball came nicely on to the bat. Pranav, standing on the orange peel, lofted it high over the mid-off boundary. 'Four!!!' yelled VIII B as Thomas, fielding there, ran to retrieve it. The last ball was faster and took Pranav by surprise. He brought his bat down quickly and the resultant edge carried to Kishore at first slip who made no mistake. Another five runs were reduced. Pranav's score was minus six, but there were six extras, so the score remained the same.

Pranav, annoyed with himself, decided to stay at the other end and sent Sumay to the pavilion. Hemant, the next batsman, walked in with a badminton racquet in his hand. Pranav handed him the pads.

'Which end?' asked the umpire.

'Eh?' Hemant looked puzzled.

'Of the bat. Are you going to hold the handle of the racquet to bat or the head? If it's the head, you'll get ten extra runs.'

'Er . . .' Hemant hadn't thought of that since he had practised holding the handle. Though the prospect of foregoing ten runs wasn't very attractive, he said, 'The handle.' A minute later, he wished he hadn't made that choice. The bowler was Thomas and he was bowling with a golf ball. The first ball was pitched short and Hemant prepared to whack it. To the shock of the batsman and the amusement of everyone, the ball went right though the net and knocked off the off stump.

'A hole?' Hemant was horrified to find he had brought the wrong racquet from home. It already had a couple of strings broken and the hard golf ball had widened the opening. Dismayed, he asked Mr Sunderlal if he could use the other end but the umpire refused firmly. 'You've already faced a ball,' he said.

Thomas was ruthlessly accurate, there was no question about it, and though Hemant tried to use the metal frame to see off the ball, he got bowled by the next two deliveries too, the ball unerringly making its passage through the hole both times. He was lucky with the super ball, though. It was a mango and Thomas lost his balance as he was about to bowl. The mango flew off his hand straight to Amar and got him neatly on the chest, splashing yellow pulp all over his shirt. Five extra runs were awarded. With great concentration, Hemant managed to get the next ball on the bottom of the racquet's frame and dispatched it to the cover boundary. He tried the same shot with the next and missed, but the ball too missed the stump by a whisker. He breathed a sigh of relief as he left with his score, as Mahesh shouted out, 'Minus 11, VIII B 106.'

The next batsman, Nitin, faced Kishore with a hockey stick. Ten runs were added immediately. Kishore had a blue sock ball with him. The ball swung quite a bit. Nitin expertly got the first ball on the stick and sent it along the ground for a single. He was beaten by the swing of the second ball, got an edge and Minu gratefully accepted the catch at first slip. The third ball was an action replay of the second, but this time, he got the middle of the stick on it and lofted it to deep mid-on where there was no fielder. By the time Jayaram chased down the ball, the batsman had taken two runs comfortably.

It was time for the super ball. Kishore gestured to the crowd, like an athlete at an international meet, to start applauding and the students obliged delightedly. Nobody even heard the umpire say, 'Papaya'. They also chanted 'tom-at-o, to-mat-o, to-mat-o' rhythmically, keeping time with the hand clapping and when this reached a crescendo, Kishore released the papaya. Nitin saw it flying to him and held the stick up defensively. By some fluke, the papaya ball landed in the centre of the curve and got stuck there without bursting.

The crowd roared with laughter. 'Howzzat!' yelled Reshmi and the close in fielders.

'My runs. Six,' asserted Nitin, turning for confirmation to Mr Sunderlal who had to make a quick decision. Nobody had reckoned with such a situation. But since the fruit hadn't cracked, the umpire signalled six runs for Nitin.

VIII B greeted the first six of the match with ear-shattering yells. Manas hooted from the pavilion, studiously avoiding Mr Jagmohan's annoyed gaze.

Kishore stomped to the bowling mark and threw a fast and furious delivery that was a blur of blue and sailed away behind Reshmi. The umpire cautioned Kishore for throwing and called it a no-ball. One extra run. Ajay went up to Kishore to calm him down. Nitin went on his knees, got the next ball on the curve of the stick and swept it to the boundary. The last ball was cut late by Nitin, a lovely shot, but equally well fielded by Ajay and there was no run. The fielders heaved a sigh of relief. Now the total was 125 and Nitin had eighteen to his name. He raised his bat in triumph and swaggered all the way to the pavilion forgetting to give the pads to the last man, Ishaan, who was walking to the crease. Ishaan had to run after him and pull him by his shirt collar to get his attention.

Kiran was the bowler for Ishaan and proudly tossed up a ball made of rubber bands. He had taken a whole evening to make it. The word went around in no time and everyone waited eagerly to see the action. Ishaan had a mosquito bat with him that he held by its handle. Mr Sunderlal didn't ask for any clarification this time. The first ball spun in fast and watching carefully, Ishaan got the middle of his bat on it and sent it straight to Amar at gully who put down the sitter. 'Way to go, Butterfingers!' shouted Tanmay of VIII B.

But Amar had the last laugh. He quickly collected the ball and as the batsmen were scrambling for a run, threw down the stumps with a direct throw. Ishaan was run out. Returning to the crease, Ishaan came dancing out to face the next delivery, misjudged the spin and missed it completely to be stumped. Minus five again. Holding the bat like a racquet now, he played a Nadal style two-handed backhand shot to the next delivery and it soared over Ajay's head to reach the boundary.

This time the super ball was indeed a tomato much to the crowd's joy, and it began the tomato chant with gusto. Ishaan got the vegetable in the centre of the bat and at the moment of impact, switched it on. There was a swish, a crackle, a splutter and some sparks. 'Roasted tomato,' announced Ishaan proudly. Mr Sunderlal came to examine the bat and thoughtlessly put his finger on the still-charged net. He immediately withdrew it with a jerk and a muttered oath. 'Shocking!' he glared at Ishaan and raised his abused finger to declare the batsman out. He removed the batteries and put them in his pocket before handing the bat back to the batsman.

Ishaan, quite unfazed, cleverly judged the spin of the next ball and nudged it to extra cover for a single. The last ball spun bizarrely and he got an edge. It flew to Reshmi but a slight touch from her carried it to Arvind at first slip. Arvind couldn't hold on to the ball, which seemed to have acquired a life of its own, but Minu leapt from third slip to take a spectacular catch. Everyone crowded around Minu who had made up for her disappointing bowling with two great catches. The match ended with 110 runs on the board. Ishaan's score was minus fifteen.

13

An Exciting Finish

VIII A needed 111 runs for a win. The players walked back to the pavilion for a five-minute drinks break. Chuhaa began to bark and Amar turned to see Bluebottle walking towards a chair in the far corner. 'Look who's here! Secondly, Bluebottle's come to watch our innings,' Amar whispered to Kiran who grinned and replied, 'Ah, but firstly someone wants a taste of his ankles.'

Pranav soon led the VIII B fielders into the grounds. Ajay and Abdul walked in without pads, helmets or gloves. 'Batsman number one–Abdul,' the umpire read out aloud from the list. 'And bowler number one is Jithin.' Abdul held a vacuum cleaner's extension tube in his hand. The umpire took one look and signalled ten runs for Abdul. Jithin, VIII B's opening bowler, went to the bowling mark. He had a rubber ball with him. Dipankar, the wicketkeeper, wore the pads the batsmen had worn earlier and a pair of boxing gloves. A rather large motorcycle half helmet with racing stickers on it that belonged to his brother sat loosely on his head.

Abdul was a stylish left-hander. A naturally gifted player with a silken touch, he always gave the impression of scoring runs effortlessly. Every opposition team dreaded him and VIII B was glad their best bowler would be bowling to him. The first ball was fast, but Abdul saw it well and got his bat to it. With a slight but sure touch he directed the ball to the cover boundary. The second ball was beautifully played but equally well fielded by Ishaan. No run. Abdul missed the third which barely cleared the top of the stumps but Dipankar, whose helmet had slid over his eyes, couldn't see it and the ball flew for four byes. Loud curses and murder threats from his teammates forced Dipankar to reluctantly part with his helmet.

The super ball was an orange. Abdul ran halfway down the pitch to get it gently and expertly on his bat and caressed it to deep fine leg without cracking it, inviting a roar of applause. 'Six!' signalled the umpire.

'Very smart. The boy's a genius,' said Mr Dinesh to Mr Jagmohan who had begun to nod off.

'Yes, yes, a marvel,' the principal woke up with a start to reply. 'Who is it?'

Unfortunately the success with the super ball brought on a lapse in concentration and Abdul got out to the last two deliveries, returning identical catches to the bowler as if he were giving him catching practice. 'VIII A total 114 and Abdul 10,' yelled Jaydev. Abdul had scored far less than was expected of him and looked so unhappy that Ajay came out to console him. Abdul then crossed over to the non-striker's end.

Ajay went to the pavilion to fetch his 'bat', his grandfather's walking stick, getting ten runs straightaway. But that was all the luck he had. Mitra was the bowler and bowling with a rubber ball, he was able to extract turn. The first ball fooled Ajay with its flight. He missed it and was bowled. He managed to loft the second to deep mid-on and Manas covered a lot of ground to take a fantastic catch. He crowed over it for a long time. The third was pitched short, and Ajay attempted to play it but the stick was too narrow and he was bowled again.

The super ball was a custard apple and Ajay, determined to make amends by getting six runs, brought his bat down to it a little too hard. It burst into pieces and flew in all directions. Minus five again. The last two deliveries, perfectly flighted, were dot balls and Ajay hung his head as he walked back with minus ten against his name. So much for all the practice. Manas rubbed salt in his wound by shouting, 'Captain knocked!' after him. The score was down to 104.

Arvind shuffled in with the tightly-rolled golf umbrella under his arm and asked, 'Ten runs, isn't it, sir, whichever end I use for batting?' The umpire didn't relish being dictated to and said curtly, 'Yes, but you can use only one end for the whole over.'

'Suits me,' Arvind grinned and took guard with the pointed end of the umbrella. Hitesh, who bowled medium pace, got ready to bowl with a multicoloured soft ball that was larger than the other balls used so far. The first ball came slowly to Arvind who, looking awkward as he clutched the long umbrella, thought he had all the time in the world to get in position but ended up missing the ball, which rolled harmlessly away from the stumps. The second ball came fast and again Arvind missed, but this time it decided to land gently on the stumps, balancing itself on the off and middle. 'Howzzat!' appealed Dipankar and all the close in fielders, but Arvind protested saying the stumps hadn't moved at all. Mr Sunderlal took a close look, then put his finger up.

'Out!' yelled VIII B in a raucous chorus. Arvind scowled and got ready for the third ball, which again was slow and almost stopped in front of him. He used the full length of the umbrella to sweep the ball to the on-side boundary, raking up sand into the face of Nitin at short leg. Nitin was livid but Arvind pretended not to notice. Spitting some sand out of his mouth, Nitin protested to the umpire who ignored him and signalled a boundary. Mr Sunderlal was a master at the art of ignoring things whenever it suited him.

The super ball, an apple this time, was rejected by the umpire for being too hard. Vishud ran in with a ripe peach to replace it. Hitesh tossed it too high. It rose in a neat curve and would have fallen with a plop at Arvind's feet, giving five easy runs, but Arvind, closely watching it, misjudged its trajectory and thought it would smack into his face. He instinctively raised his umbrella as protection and got a touch to the fruit that rose a little and fell, bursting at his feet like an apologetic offering.

'Peach of a ball!' shouted Manas.

Arvind had lost five runs and in anger jumped up and down on the remains of the fruit.

'Haha,' Mr Hiran laughed. 'Reminds me of Miandad's famous frog leaps,' he commented.

'Me and Dad's?' Ms Susan looked puzzled and sighing, Mr Hiran explained that Javed Miandad was once Pakistan's key batsman and during the 1992 India-Pakistan World Cup match in Sydney, India's wicketkeeper Kiran More annoyed him so much by his jumping and appealing that he finally put up an exaggerated imitation of the wicketkeeper's antics. 'Oh? So sweet!' Ms Susan gushed. Exasperated, Mr Hiran turned his attention back to the game.

Hitesh's next delivery was rather high and Arvind decided to move away. But accidentally his finger pressed the button at the head of the umbrella and it opened without a warning, sending the ball which landed on it back like a boomerang to the bowler who, not expecting this odd return catch, put it down. Arvind flung the open umbrella towards first slip and ran for a single with Abdul responding eagerly, but Hitesh, Pranav and Dipankar appealed to the umpire who promptly raised his finger and said, 'Out!'

Arvind protested angrily. 'It was an accident.'

'You used an open umbrella to play the ball; that's not allowed,' Mr Sunderlal was firm.

A furious Arvind lashed at the last delivery that flew back to Hitesh. This time the bowler accepted the catch gratefully. Arvind had scored minus six and VIII A's score was 98.

Jayaram was in next and his bat was his cousin's toy guitar. He wondered if Manas was going to bowl to him and was relieved to find Milosh's name announced by the umpire. Milosh went to his bowling mark with a tennis ball. The guitar had a string or two broken. Holding the bat with one hand around the head stock and the other gripping the neck, the batsman was ready. Milosh was known for his accuracy and the guitar received the first ball with a hollow sound as Jayaram played forward defensive to it. The second ball was a half volley which Jayaram whacked to the cover fielder's head with a boom, sending him cowering fearfully instead of fielding it. The ball raced to the boundary. Milosh took a long run up to bowl the next delivery and overstepped as the ball left his hand. Jayaram, delighted to see a full toss coming his way, stretched his guitar to loft the ball only to see it disappear into its sound hole with a thud.

'No-ball!' declared the umpire.

'No ball, sir,' said Jayaram.

'That's what I said.' Mr Sunderlal sounded annoyed.

'No ball, sir, ball's lost in the guitar,' explained Jayaram, fishing inside the sound hole for it. Mr Sunderlal was exasperated. He wondered, for the hundredth time, why he had agreed to umpire this crazy match.

The ball was recovered with some difficulty and the next delivery landed on the strings. Twang! The guitar protested off-key as the ball curled into the hands of Mitra at first slip. The super ball was a tomato. Mr Sunderlal examined it and, satisfied it was soft enough, handed it back to the bowler. 'Tomato-oh-oh-ooo!' the crowd chanted. Mitra tried to flight the 'ball' and Jayaram this time deliberately got it into the sound hole and then overturned the guitar on the ground. The tomato tumbled out, unscathed.

'Six!' said Abdul from the other end.

'Foul play! Out!' the bowler and all the fielders appealed.

The umpire thought for a while, then signalled a six. All the fielders surrounded him in protest, but he refused to overturn his decision. 'If the batsman has negotiated the ball successfully without cracking it, he gets six runs. That's what the rules say and that's what happened now.'

Jayaram was so pleased with this he didn't concentrate on the next ball and hurriedly brought the guitar down only to play on. He played the last ball to deep third man and managed a couple of runs. 'Jayaram, two runs and VIII A's total is 101!' announced Mahesh. 'Ten more runs to win.'

The atmosphere grew tense. Everything now depended on the last batsman, Amar, and the last bowler. 'It's Manas for you, Butter, be careful,' cautioned Jayaram. All his teammates crowded around

176

him with advice. They were glad that he was facing Manas. Of all the players, he was the best choice to counter Manas. Ajay was relieved that his hunch to reserve Amar for the last in case Manas was also intended for that slot had worked.

'The score's 101, Butter,' Kiran reminded him when he picked up his bat. 'Keep that in mind and be alert. That idiot will have a bag of tricks with him.'

A generous round of applause accompanied Amar all the way to the crease. Vishud handed Manas the basket containing the balls with a broad wink. Abdul, still at the non-striker's end, saw it and went to warn Amar.

'I think they are up to something. Be on your guard, Butter.'

Amar nodded as he got ready to take guard. The umpire took one look at the ball Manas held out to him and protested. 'What nonsense is this?' he asked angrily.

'Where does it say in the rules the ball must be hard? We only have specifications for the super ball,' Manas retorted, holding up his ball—a thick balloon filled with water. He had a few more in the basket.

'A water ball!' announced Jaydev. 'What a ball!'

'Foul! Cheaters!' VIII A's indignant cries rent the air. 'Skulduggery!' shouted Kishore as Ajay ran to the pitch. Pranav and the rest of the VIII B team were already surrounding the umpire, protesting the ball wasn't breaking any rules.

The umpire was in a dilemma, wondering what decision to make when Amar, to everyone's surprise, said he was game for it. The situation greatly appealed to his sense of mischief. Relieved, Mr Sunderlal signalled for play to continue. Ajay went back to the pavilion, looking worried.

The whole school was on its feet now, not wishing to miss this unique tussle between the bat and the shivering ball. Manas had obviously practised hard, for the first ball, a full toss, came wobbling in a high arc straight to Amar. Amar hit it hard and it went up into the silly mid-on region. Jithin took a running catch but it jiggled out of his hands and he couldn't stop himself from stepping on it. The water ball burst. Amar and Abdul kept running until Jithin realized they would stop only when the ball was back with the bowler. He hurriedly picked up the pieces of balloon and ran to Manas. Amar had run three. 104!

The next ball was wide. Amar should have left it alone but hungry for runs, he chased it, managing only to loft it into the hands of Pranav who ran to get into position for the catch only to drop the ball and inadvertently give it a kick too. There was a loud groan from VIII B as Sumay, sprinting to stop the ball, fell and pushed it over the boundary line. VIII A delightedly screamed '108!' Before the third delivery could fall with a plop right in front of the batsman, which was Manas's intention, Amar came forward, scooped it in a neat sweep and sent it over the wicketkeeper's head for an outrageous boundary. 'Terrific dilscoop!' exclaimed Abdul appreciatively. 'DILSCOOOOOOP!!!' yelled the crowd. The score was now 112 and Amar waited for the super ball. He knew Manas would try something new here. He was a little worried, for his bat was wobbling a little more, as if it wished to match the ball.

The umpire examined the ball and said, 'Orange.' Amar watched Manas like a hawk and noticed him drop his handkerchief near the basket, stoop to pick it up and under that pretext, quickly switch fruits. Realizing instantly that Manas meant to throw a rotten fruit on his face, Amar decided to pre-empt him. Unmindful of losing runs, Amar ran forward as Manas released the rotten orange, got it on the meat of his bat and smashed it with great force right back on Manas's face. It burst into pieces, the juice splashed into Manas's eyes while some pulp went into his nose and mouth. VIII A cheered wildly even though the umpire signalled out and the total fell to 107. Manas coughed, spluttered and rubbed his eyes and face with his handkerchief. His teammates were also heartened by this sight, hiding smiles of satisfaction when they saw him spit out orange pips.

The angry ball that was flung next was left well alone by Amar, and Dipankar leaped athletically to his right to collect it before it could go for byes. The score remained on 107 and now it was the last ball. The team needed four runs to win.

'Go for it, Butter!' yelled VIII A. 'You can do it.'

'Get him out, Manas,' shouted the rival class. The others watched eagerly. This was just the nail-biting finish they had hoped for.

Amar looked sternly down at his unsteady bat, willing it to cooperate in his plan. He expected Manas to bowl a yorker and that was exactly what he did. Amar came forward lithely and got his bat to the ball. Wielding his bat like a mace, his body in perfect position, he swung his arms around to execute Dhoni's patented helicopter shot so perfectly the ball went flying over the boundary for a four. An enterprising class VII boy ran forward, pocketed the water ball and went straight home.

But something else also went soaring up. The blade of Amar's bat had separated from the handle and flew towards the pavilion. And an object that gleamed and shone dropped out of the airborne bat.

Nobody noticed Bluebottle leap up and run on to the field. Abdul had already lifted Amar off his feet when the rest of his teammates rushed to join in shouldering the hero who held the handle aloft, a pleased grin on his face. The whole school clapped and cheered loudly. From the heights, Amar suddenly noticed Bluebottle pick something up and race away with the rest of his bat.

At the same moment Mr Rohan cried out, 'Stop!' and pushed through the crowd to give chase to Bluebottle who already had a head start. Out of nowhere a barking Chuhaa came on the scene, determined to become a biting Chuhaa and chew on

Bluebottle's ankles. For some time utter confusion reigned on the grounds. Nobody knew what the barks and shouts meant and who was chasing whom or why.

Chuhaa finally managed to stop Bluebottle's incredible sprinting by getting his teeth firmly on the policeman's left trouser leg. Rajan had just about stopped Chuhaa from proceeding to make a meal of Bluebottle's ankles when Mr Rohan came panting up, followed by a serious-looking bearded man who had been among the spectators.

'Ah, caught you red-handed!' said Mr Rohan to Bluebottle, snatching the bat from him. Amar and his friends, who had also reached there and were watching the dramatic happenings, looked astounded. 'Policeman, indeed! We've been keeping an eye on you for sometime now. You are under arrest,' Mr Rohan pronounced in a stern voice. Turning to the man who had joined him, clearly a policeman in plainclothes, or mufti, as Thomas would have been quick to point out, Rohan sir said, 'Madhukar, search this man and take him away.'

'Yes, sir,' said Mr Madhukar.

The search yielded two diamonds in Bluebottle's right trouser pocket, the ones that had fallen out of the bat. Handing them over to Mr Rohan, Mr Madhukar led Bluebottle, still looking fearfully at a barking Chuhaa, out of the school.

'Diamonds?' Amar looked incredulous. 'Inside my bat?'

'Yes, and there are more in it.' Mr Rohan shook the bat hard and some more sparkling stones fell out. 'This is where the Jewel Thief had hidden the stolen stuff.'

Amar looked overawed by this information. 'And you are a police insp . . .?'

'. . . ector. Yes.' Mr Rohan nodded. Mr Jagmohan's voice was heard asking everyone to settle down for the prize distribution. 'Now let's go for the prize-giving ceremony. Keep quiet about all this.' The boys were forced to curb their curiosity for the time being and obediently followed Mr Rohan to the pavilion.

No mention was made about the nabbing of the Sporting Thief. Mr Jagmohan paid tribute to Colonel Nadkarni before congratulating the teams on a wonderful game of Crack It. He then invited Mr Dinesh Nadkarni to give away the medals to the winners and the runners-up. Mr Dinesh Nadkarni praised the players for a keenly-fought match, the kind of contest his late uncle would have relished. The cardboard boxes were opened and the winners were also given a bat each while VIII B got balls. Ajay generously donated his team's bats to the school and VIII B was forced to follow suit. Amar was everyone's choice for the man of the match award—all his runs had come off his wobbly bat that had won its battle with the wobbly ball, and he had taken his team to victory in style. The prize for his 'sparkling performance' as Mr Dinesh whispered to him with a twinkle in his eyes while placing it on his head was a smart blue cap.

14

Under-Fifty vs Under-Fifteen

Amar was polishing off his breakfast when Mr Kishen, who was as usual buried behind the paper, exclaimed, 'Goodness, Amar! You're in the papers today, or at least your hands and your broken bat are.'

'What!' Both Amar and his mother immediately stretched their hands for the paper. Mr Kishen held up the paper to show them the picture but kept his hold on it.

'Wonder who took the picture,' Amar commented. 'Must have caught it on a mobile phone camera. I wish whoever it was had got my face too.'

'I'm sure it was there, Amar, but they must have wisely edited it out. They didn't want to ruin the photo.' Rajeev Kishen ignored his son's indignant protest and continued, 'Listen. The headlines are, "Crack It Cracks Cracking Missing Jewels Case." Well, really! The headlines these days! The report goes on to clarify many things that mystified you, Amar. "The Jewel Thief case and the Sporting Thief case that had baffled the police department's best brains . . ." ahem! ". . . for more than two months now have finally been solved. The police got the breakthrough when, during the course of an innovative cricket match called Crack It in Green Park School, the bat used by the vice-captain Amar Kishen broke when he played a vigorous helicopter shot and it went on to rain precious stones." Haha, rained, indeed, precious shower, that. How many stones were there, Amar?'

'Just a few, but go on, Dad.' Amar was impatient.

'"The thief had stuffed the jewels into a fake bat and was taking it to his accomplice when he realized the police were after him. He hid it in the first shed he passed and soon after he was arrested. He wasn't able to tell his accomplice where he had hidden them, since his mobile phone was immediately confiscated. Apparently he had only hinted earlier it was in some cricket gear, wishing it to be a surprise. The accomplice now began stealing cricket equipment and burning it after a thorough search."'

'So the Jewel Thief and the Sporting Thief were connected, after all!' Amar looked pleased. 'Should've guessed Bluebottle was the accomplice. To think we almost forcibly made him the policeman and dragged him into our school!'

'"When the Jewel Thief, whose name is Subhash Gaurav, escaped from prison last week, he executed another daring robbery—the priceless Safed Haathi diamond was stolen from Seth Sitaram's safe, as reported earlier. Gaurav was again arrested but has refused to divulge the whereabouts of the diamond. He told the police he had dropped it while fleeing from them. Mr Rohan Rai, the detective inspector investigating the case, was on the school grounds when the jewels stolen earlier were discovered. The Sporting Thief, Viswas Sarath, a small-time theatre actor who is the accomplice of the Jewel Thief, was trying to run away with the jewels when he was arrested."'

'Theatre actor!' Amar interrupted. 'No wonder he was able to improvise so quickly. Brilliant!'

His father glared at him and continued, '"Once the Safed Haathi is recovered, the case will be closed. The police think the chances of obtaining valuable information from Viswas Sarath are dim since he appears to be in the dark about this diamond too. The Commissioner has announced awards for all those who helped solve the case."'

'So we're getting an award, yaay!' Amar raised both his hands in a celebratory gesture, sending the puri in his hand flying to a corner of the dining room. 'Oops!' He rose to pick it up.

'Oh, Amar!' said his mother, exasperated. 'No, don't bother. I'll do that. You'd better rush. It's getting late.'

'Oh no, so it is! Wonder what Princi will say at the assembly.' Kiran's voice was heard calling his name and with a 'Bye, Dad, Ma!' flung over his shoulder, Amar picked up his bag and ran out, the door thudding shut behind him.

'That boy!' Mr Kishen shook his head and went back to reading the newspaper.

⌒

At school, Mr Jagmohan had received an email from Mr Vijay:

Clean Bowled, Butterfingers!

My dear Jagmohan, isn't it wonderful that Green Park School should be in all the newspapers? And that a student of ours should have helped solve a difficult case? Is Amar the same boy who wrote out that proposal for the cricket match? Smart fellow—you should be very proud of him. And listen, I've an idea. Why not reward the students by asking them to play a cricket match against the teachers instead of the other match? The teachers can then put up a very good team and pit their strength against a strong school team. Will be a spectacular affair. Let me know what you think of this idea asap.
With regards
Vijay

'Ha!' Mr Jagmohan exclaimed to himself. 'I've got an idea too, Mr Vijay.' Mr Jagmohan could think on his seat and immediately shot off a reply:

Brilliant idea, Mr Vijay. The boys will be thrilled and the teachers will be happy too, since only those who really enjoy cricket and know the game well need play now. Anyway, thanks to all the new rules, the teachers are now leading active, healthy lives. They use the gym regularly, play games and enjoy what they are doing. Why don't we have an Under-Fifty vs Under-Fifteen match? This would be a fitting commemorative match for Colonel Nadkarni since the annual match Colonel Nadkarni sponsored was also for the Under-Fifteen students. Let me know what you think.
Regards
Jagmohan

He got a two-liner immediately.

Wonderful! Make arrangements to hold this match on
Monday. The trustees and I will be there.

Mr Jagmohan chuckled. His fiftieth birthday fell on
Sunday, so he knew he wouldn't be picked. 'What a
brainwave!' He kept congratulating himself.

He looked euphoric when he faced the school at
the assembly. 'Princi looks like a cat that's eaten a big
fat canary,' whispered Amar to Eric.

Instead of glaring, the principal looked benignly at
him. 'Amar has every right to be excited and therefore
distracted,' he said over the mike. 'He's a hero. Give
him a big hand!'

After the students almost brought some branches down
with their shouting and clapping, he continued, 'Thanks to
him, a difficult case was solved and our school is in the
papers. Mr Vijay sent a mail suggesting that instead of a
match between the teachers, as planned earlier, we could
have one between the teachers and the students—The
Under-Fifty vs the Under-Fifteen—on Monday.'

The students were thrilled, especially those in
the Under-Fifteen team and the teachers, hearing the
announcement in the staffroom, were pleasantly
surprised. After some more cheering the students went
to their classes.

But something was troubling Amar and his friends
and as they reached the class, the person they wanted

to see passed by. 'Rohan sir, er, Inspector Rohan sir, we have something to ask you,' said Amar.

The teacher smiled and stopped. 'Call me Rohan sir—I like that. Yes, I know. I shouldn't have fooled you and the school like this. But it wasn't really fooling. I am a qualified teacher too. Physics is indeed my subject and Mr Jagmohan understands. I have another week to hunt for Safed Haathi, but whether I succeed or not, I have to rejoin duty after that. I liked it very much here, but I have to go back. After the match, of course.'

'That's nice, sir,' said Amar. 'Er, not that you're going,' he hurriedly added, 'but that you'll be here for the match, and play too, we hope. But sir, we have something else to ask you. If you were after the thief, why didn't you examine the bat that was in your own shed?'

'What bat?' Mr Rohan looked puzzled. 'There was no bat in my shed.'

'What! But sir, we got it from your shed.'

'Nonsense!' Mr Rohan looked a little irritated. 'I asked you to take whatever you wanted from the shed but I'd already searched it thoroughly.'

The students looked at one another and the same thought struck all of them. 'Ironman!' exclaimed Amar, Eric and Kishore at the same time.

'What Ironman?' Mr Rohan looked annoyed but the students saw Mr Shyam approach the class and quickly saying, 'Thank you, sir,' they ran in.

'Marvellous sign language experts you and Kishore are!' Eric teased the two culprits in a whisper. 'Wonder where Ironman got the bat from.'

That evening, while the rest of the team practised cricket, Amar, Eric and Kishore decided to visit Ironman. They saw Mr Dinesh Nadkarni about to enter his house as they came up. On seeing them, he stopped and waited for them. 'So how's our hero dealing with the fame?' He greeted them with a broad smile and patted Amar on his back. Amar's prize cap promptly fell off.

'Head's getting too big for his cap,' said Kishore, picking it up.

Amar grinned and asked, 'Mr Dinesh, did you hear the latest? The Colonel Nadkarni memorial match is now to be played between the teachers and the students—Under-Fifty vs Under-Fifteen. Mr Sunderlal is very happy. He can now choose an awesome team.'

'Really? That'd be very exciting. I was planning to watch the other match anyway. But why the change?'

'Mr Vijay was so pleased with us for getting the school into the papers that he wanted to reward us,' explained Amar. 'Rumours are that Mr Jagmohan suggested the Under Fifty bit because his fiftieth birthday falls this Sunday and the match is on Monday. He wants to get out of playing it. Smart Princi! But I don't think Sunderlal sir would have picked him anyway.'

Mr Dinesh laughed, then grew serious. 'What did you say, the match's this Monday? I thought it was the Monday after. Oh no! Then I'll miss it.'

He explained he was leaving that evening for Switzerland on a business trip. 'It's for a week. I thought I'd return in time for the match.'

The disappointed expressions on the faces of the boys mirrored his. But almost immediately Amar said, 'Never mind, Mr Dinesh. We'll send you an email about it. Kishore used to send emails to Colonel Uncle too when he missed matches.'

Mr Dinesh brightened. 'That'd be really nice, and make it lively. I'll look forward to it. Here's my card. My mail id's on it. Bye and good luck!'

'Thanks, Mr Dinesh. Bye!' the boys chorused. 'Have a safe flight and say hello to Roger Federer and his double set of twins for us,' Amar added. Mr Dinesh laughed and waved as he closed the gate.

The boys now raced to Ironman's house. He wasn't there, but his wife was. Kishore had just begun by saying, 'We are friends of Ironman . . .' in sign language when she turned to Amar and said, 'Tut, tut, poor boy, he too can't hear or speak, just like my husband. How sad! But what's he saying? I can't follow him. Which sign language is he using?'

The boys laughed. 'Kishore is an idiot. A perfect fool. Our teachers have given up teaching him the standard sign language. He's invented his own and no one can make head or tail of it. Forget him,' said Eric. Kishore spluttered and glowered at him. 'We wanted to meet your husband to ask about a bat he gave us.'

'Oh, I remember. He said some boys had no bat to play cricket and he felt sorry for them. So I told him to give them the bat he got from a shed that was being pulled down. The owner was putting up a new house there and had asked him to clear the shed. Why?'

'No, no, we came to thank him,' said Amar hurriedly. 'Tell him we played with his bat and won the match. We got new bats as a prize and want to give him one.'

'Oh, he'll be thrilled. It's very nice of you. He really wants to learn to play cricket and play for India under Dhoni.'

'Don't worry, we'll coach him. We'll bring the bat next week. Bye!'

She waved cheerfully and gave poor Kishore a sympathetic hug. He pulled himself away before she could give him a light peck on his cheek. The other two controlled their laughter and ran for their lives with Kishore charging like a mad bull after them. A rough and tumble later, they sat down, panting.

'So Ironman got his hands on the bat quite by chance. But what luck he gave it to us!' exclaimed Amar.

'Yes, but how'll you give him a new bat?' asked Kishore. 'We donated all our bats to school.'

'We'll ask Sunderlal sir for one, of course. You're so dumb, Kishore!' Amar laughed. Kishore glared angrily, then laughed too.

Now that the bat mystery was solved, they gave all their attention to the match that had only three days to go.

On Monday evening, Mr Dinesh Nadkarni received the following email from Kishore:

Dear Mr Dinesh

Unbelievable excitement here! Hold on to your chair, sir, and read on . . .

It was Monday, the day of the match, and guess who came to class? Arjun, in person, quite unrecognizable, with short hair, no earring and a new husky voice. Ajay greeted him with, 'Will you be wicketkeeper?' 'No, man, no sports for a week, doctor's orders,' he whispered, looking so unhappy Amar cracked a few jokes to cheer him up and laughed at all of them himself. In the morning Mr Jagmohan grudgingly declared a half holiday, courtesy Mr Vijay's wish. The junior school was sent home and boy, were they mad!

We were all asked to be on the grounds at 1.45 so that the match could begin at 2 p.m. We went by 1.40 and found Sunderlal sir in a flap. The new cricketing gear, purchased with the money given as reward, had arrived but without wicketkeeping gloves. That reminded us about Arjun's gloves and Reshmi took over. Here's an interlude of how the conversation went . . .

Reshmi: Oh, Arjun, we have bad news for you. We didn't know how to break it. The Sporting Thief burnt your stinking gloves too, along with the rest of the sports gear he stole from our school.

We thought Arjun would faint, with no help from his gloves, or have a fit, but surprisingly he didn't turn

a hair (he doesn't have much of it now, anyway, haha).
Now get ready for the next surprise, Mr Dinesh.

Arjun: He can't have. Here they are.

And he fished them out of his bag, like a conjuror
pulling out a couple of smelly rabbits from his hat.
Sensation. Amar held his nose and took two quick steps
backwards.

Sunderlal sir raised his eyebrows in that special
questioning manner he has patented.

Arjun (pointing to Mr Rohan): I heard sir say that
he hoped the Sporting Thief would steal all the sports
gear. So I took my gloves home that night. I didn't want
to lose my precious gloves.

Ajay (looking relieved and happy): Good for you,
Arjun. Smelly gloves are better than no gloves at all.
Amar has agreed to be wicketkeeper, so he'll bear them,
I mean, wear them.

Amar looked as if he had swallowed something awful
and used the thumb and index finger of his left hand to
take them from Arjun. End of interlude.

Mahesh, our head boy was the umpire, and strutted
to the pitch at exactly 2 p.m. looking very important.
Sunderlal sir and Ajay soon walked out to toss. Ajay
later said he was so overawed at having our PT master
beside him as the rival captain that when sir tossed
the coin and he had to call, Ajay said, 'Hails, I mean
teads, I mean . . .' He got thoroughly confused and
they had to toss again. This time he said sternly,
'Heads.' The coin circled around merrily for a while,

lengthening the suspense and finally fell on its head. 'It's tails!' announced Mahesh. The pitch appeared so full of runs, Sunderlal sir naturally elected to bat.

Ajay led us to the field with Amar holding his hands out, trying his best to put as much distance as possible between his nose and Arjun's gloves. Hiran sir and Ojhas sir opened the batting and saw off Jithin, who was as hostile as Dale Steyn, no less. They weren't troubled by anyone else and Ojhas sir was especially flamboyant. They piled on the runs, helped also by Amar. Our Butterfingers was at his butterfingered best. He dropped a sitter and a difficult half chance, allowed byes and leg byes, missed a stumping and collected so ineptly a ball that would have run Hiran sir out that it went for four overthrows. He was obviously uncomfortable behind the stumps and we made things worse by calling him all kinds of names, including Butterfingers, of course.

He finally redeemed himself by taking a diving catch off Eric's bowling to send Ojhas sir to the pavilion. It was in the seventh over and Ojhas sir had scored twenty-eight runs. The teachers gave him a huge ovation! I've never seen them so animated. Ms Naaz came next and Eric chivalrously sent a slow, straight delivery that was dispatched smartly to the boundary. It put an end to his gallantry and a clever off break got her plumb lbw. Everyone appealed. 'Out!' said Mahesh, putting his finger up. She smiled sweetly at him, said 'Thank you' and walked away.

Now Sunderlal sir arrived at the crease and this was what we'd been dreading because he knows every bowler's action inside out. The runs began to flow freely, like champagne out of a bottle. Sunderlal sir was at his elegant best, quite like V.V.S. Laxman, and showed the same commitment to the team's cause. Soon the 50 and then the 75 was up. Amar dropped an easy chance given by Hiran sir off the last ball of the penultimate over. The bowler Mitra almost bit Butter's head off. Amar looked miserable as he went over to the other end.

'Anything wrong?' asked Sunderlal sir.

'My gloves are hurting me,' mumbled Amar. This brief exchange distracted Sunderlal sir who edged the next delivery rocketed in by Jithin. Amar flew to his left to bring off a sensational catch.

'Great catch!' Sunderlal sir complimented Amar as he left to thunderous applause. Sir had made thirty-eight and the total was 111. Rohan sir walked a little nervously to the crease and as the fielders continued to celebrate, Amar felt a sharp pain in his right hand. 'Ouch! Something's bitten me!' He pulled off his right glove and something fell out. Rohan sir picked it up.

Amar's finger was bleeding like a leaking tap and muttering something to Mahesh, Rohan sir walked quickly back to the pavilion. We bandaged the wound with Minu's kerchief, by far the cleanest on offer. Rohan sir returned with Sunderlal sir and after they tied a proper bandage on Butter's finger, our wicketkeeper stuffed his hand once again into Arjun's glove, crinkled his nose and was ready for play.

Rohan sir, looking suddenly confident, smashed two boundaries and when the innings closed, he and Hiran sir were unbeaten on nine and thirty-two respectively and the final score was 121 for 3. Extras 10, all through Butter's generosity.

We had to score at more than eight an over to win. We began confidently with Ajay and Arvind scoring fluently. But then Rohan sir came to bowl, and wasn't he a revelation! It was a superb display of spin bowling and yes, hold your breath, he got unbelievable assistance from the fielders. Who'd have believed our teachers were capable of such athleticism? You really missed a good thing—it was such a treat to see them run, jump and leap like mountain goats and glide, slide, catch and throw like Jonty Rhodes. Awesome display. They were obviously enjoying their cricket, even Hiran sir, their wicketkeeper who was wearing Arjun's gloves. Thanks to his faulty olfactory system, he couldn't smell a thing.

We were getting the runs but losing wickets too. It was a total team effort from us and a team effort from the opposition too, with Rohan sir getting the wickets and the rest helping him get them. Ms Naaz, who I suspect they selected so that the gentler sex is represented, actually took a brilliant catch to get rid of Abdul and then said, 'Sorry!'

When Rohan sir came to bowl the last over, we were 116 for 8, needing six to win. Jithin and Mitra were at the crease with an injured Amar, who had already chewed off half his bandage, to come in as last man. Jithin, who was facing Rohan sir, played and missed the first two deliveries and nervously lofted the third straight into the hands of Ojhas sir at short mid-on. Amar walked to the crease and took guard with shouts of 'Butter! Butterfingers!' ringing in his ears. The fourth ball banged straight into his injured finger and he dropped the bat with a cry of pain. He took his time getting ready to face the fifth delivery. Six runs still required. The spectators took up the chant of 'Butter! Sixer!' but also applauded wildly when Rohan sir went to his bowling mark. Gritting his teeth, Amar put all his strength into smashing the next delivery that spun away from the off stump to the third man boundary for a four. 'Beauty!' shouted the students. The teachers groaned.

We needed two to win and the ground went silent. Ajay wouldn't watch. Mr Jagmohan, the trustees and the teachers were half out of their chairs. Rohan sir ambled in and bowled a flighted ball that appeared to be on leg and middle. But it drifted and pitched outside the leg stump, on a perfect length. It broke sharply and headed for the off stump. How Amar, who was drawn to the front foot, managed to step back and bring his bat down in time to squeeze it past gully I'll never know, but he did. Perfect ball and perfectly he faced it. He ran like a rabbit for a run. But of course he had to trip and give everyone a heart attack. Luckily it was a fortuitous tripping, for the resultant leap helped him land dramatically on the line, beating Sunderlal sir's superb throw by a millimetre. Butter's bat flew from his hand and would have decapitated our beloved PT sir if he hadn't leapt nimbly out of harm's way. Now the whole school leapt to its feet in relief. You'd think we had kangaroos on the grounds, the amount of leaping and jumping that was going on!

The game ended in a tie—a fitting result for an awesome match, and everyone went wild. 'It was the ball of the tournament, worthy of Shane Warne,' commended Amar as he shook Rohan sir's hand. 'But you played it as deftly as Dravid,' praised Rohan sir, patting him on the back. And this mutual admiration society went on complimenting each other till the prize-giving ceremony.

Before handing out the prizes, Mr Vijay waxed eloquent on the success of his Good Health Programme. This was his theme for quite a bit. Just as we had begun to doze off, he switched tracks and said he had never watched a better match in his life. He wondered how the trophy could be shared. He looked significantly at Ajay, who immediately piped up with a, 'No problem, sir.' We think (he never asked any of us) the Cup should be given to the Under-Fifty team since they had lost only three wickets to our nine.' Mr Vijay looked relieved. We thought it was fair enough. The trophy will certainly brighten the dull staffroom. Sunderlal sir was all smiles when he received it; so was Rohan sir when he got the Man of the Match trophy for his phenomenal nine wickets, and so were the teachers and all of us when we got our individual trophies—there were only smiles for miles around. Even Princi forgot to glare, and, instead, gave what looked suspiciously like a smile, a rarest of rare sights.

And now Mr Dinesh, read very carefully. Here comes the grand finale, the icing on the cake. Mr Vijay had asked the teams to stay back for tea with the principal and the trustees. We were delighted; we could have eaten the proverbial horse. We were eyeing the spread greedily when some strangers descended on us. Rohan sir now took over. 'These are press reporters,' he announced. Hugging his Man of the Match trophy, he first paid special tribute to 'the late Colonel Nadkarni, so well beloved of everybody that unique matches were held in his memory. I'd have loved to meet him,' he said. He went on, 'I'm especially grateful because I've been able to conquer my fear of playing cricket, a game I love. My special thanks to Amar and the rest for that!'

Amar beamed, and dropped his trophy. The rest of us only beamed.

'What do you think bit you, Amar?' Rohan sir asked. Amar was busy picking up his trophy and didn't answer.

'This!' he said, and dramatically held out a stone that shone. 'Safed Haathi.' He paused. Everyone responded with incredulous looks and exclamations of astonishment. Rohan sir looked gratified. 'Yes, the lost diamond, the Safed Haathi, has been found. I must congratulate the two instrumental in finding it—Amar

Kishen and Arjun, who's gone home. Finally, we can close the case.'

'But how did it get into the glove?' Mr Vijay asked.

'I think Subhash Gaurav, the Jewel Thief, was hiding in the school's shed,' said Rohan sir. 'He probably stuffed the diamond deep into a glove that was right at the back of the cupboard. He was arrested after that, but the next evening Arjun took the gloves home. That night the Sporting Thief, Viswas Sarath, stole the school's sports gear but found nothing. It needed a cricket match and Amar's misery behind the stumps to discover the diamond. In the end it was Amar who, to use cricket terminology, clean bowled the Jewel Thief!'

Our Butterfingers blushed and once again dropped his trophy as we applauded. Oh, Mr Dinesh, after that it was a diwali of camera flashes. We all gave so many interviews, it was awesome. Tomorrow Amar and Arjun's stinking gloves will be in all the papers. I'll send you the links. Mr Vijay's over the moon—he can't believe Green Park School's made it to the newspapers yet again!

How we all missed Colonel Uncle! Wish he had been there. He'd have enjoyed the match and all that happened after. And we wish you had been present too. But I hope this mail has helped.

We'll fill you in with minor details when you come back home.

Warm regards

Kishore

P.S. As we left, Rohan sir told us we would receive another reward. 'More cricket gear, I suppose,' Amar commented. 'But let's hope this time it includes the wicketkeeper's gloves too. Arjun's gloves have been taken away by the police as evidence. Finally, RIP.

Mr Dinesh Nadkarni burst out laughing.

Acknowledgements

They say acknowledgements have of late become as gushing as Oscar Awards speeches—everybody under the sun is profusely thanked. But let me gush just a little for I truly mean what I say.

During the course of my book's journey, from its germinal stage to the finished product, I was privileged to have worked with three editors. Sohini Mitra started the process, Niyati Dhuldhoya took over from her and in the final phase Mimi Basu joined in. All three were very supportive and a joy to work with. I am most grateful to Niyati and Mimi for their meticulous and skilful editing of the manuscript, their comments and their invaluable suggestions that helped give the book its final shape. We had many interesting discussions and I especially cherish the sapota-chikoo debate I had with them, but of course the significance of the fruit will be clear only when you read the book.

My heartfelt gratitude to my good friends Sankar Krishnan, Nayanika Krishnan and Sreelatha Nair for their inputs and their perceptive comments which were of immense help to me.

Though my deep indebtedness to the two men in my life—my husband and my son—goes without saying, I can't help saying it. Special thanks to my husband who keeps my morale high by making me believe every book I write is the best ever and to my son for holding similar views as well as for his long-distance encouragement and support.

Finally, a big thank you to my relatives, friends, students, well-wishers, readers and Butterfingers fans for their love and backing . . .

Read more in Puffin

Howzzat Butterfingers!
by Khyrunnisa.A

Watch out! With Butterfingers around, nothing and no one is safe! Amar Kishen is called Butterfingers by his parents, friends and teachers. Books, balls, bats, people, anything can go flying when Butter is around.

As school term begins, the cricket team, of which Butter is appointed the vice-captain, has its task cut out—it has to win the Colonel Nadkarni Under-Fifteen Inter-School Limited Overs Cricket Trophy. The team starts practising in earnest, but disasters follow in quick succession. The star all-rounder breaks his hand; the captain has his fifteenth birthday too soon; and their arch-rivals, Blossoms School, do the unthinkable— they include girls in their team! Worse, Green Park is going to lose its playground. Now it's up to Amar to lead the team to victory and save the day. But can he?

All this and more keep Amar and his team on their toes. Will they win the coveted trophy and save their school's grounds—or will it slip from their grasp like a classic Butterfingers catch?

Read more in Puffin

Goal, Butterfingers!
by Khyrunnisa.A

Butterfingers is back, and ready to strike!

Amar Kishen or Butterfingers, as he is popularly called, has a penchant for dropping things—he can send books, bags, balls, even people flying just by touching them!

Obsessed with football, Amar comes up with a brilliant plan—a school football tournament where each class will play as a different 'country'. And like with all Butterfingers' plans, this too is doomed to run into obstacles. First there are more girls in school (meaning, more trouble!), then there is the new English teacher, Sourpuss, who hates football and to top it all off, Princi hands out match bans over an innocent protest rally!

With things hitting rock-bottom, will Amar's class finally lift the 'World Cup'? Full of action and adventure, the second book in the Butterfingers series will make you double over following the hilarious exploits of Amar and his friends.